JAK THE GIANT HEALER

FAIRELLE BOOK EIGHT

REBEKAH R. GANIERE

FALLEN ANGEL PRESS

DEDICATION

For Niki and Grace, my partners in crime.

NEWSLETTER

Fairelle

Tanah Darah

Shaidan

Wolvenglen

Daemon Wastelands

Rift

Sage's
Hideout

Ruins

Snow's
Cottage

Volkzene

Westfall

Belle's Cottage

Morlain

Gwyn Manor

Abandoned Castle

Ville De Fee

Zelle's Tower

Draak Land

Ryna's Lake

Wizard Towers

Vedenalla

PROLOGUE

I n the year 200, in the city of Pereum, the heart of
Fairelle, King Isodor lay on his deathbed. With all of
Fairelle united under his banner, his four sons vied for
the crown. One by one the brothers called forth a djinn
named Xereus from Shaidan, the daemon realm, to grant a
single wish. But Xereus tricked the brothers, twisting their
wishes.

The eldest wished to forever be bloodthirsty in battle,
and was thus transformed into a Vampire. The second
wished for the unending loyalty of his men, and was turned
into a Werewolf. The third asked for the ability to manipu-
late the elements of Fairelle; he became physically weak but
mighty in magick, a Fae. And the last asked to rule the sea.
A Nereid.

When the king died, each brother took a piece of
Fairelle for himself and waged war for control of the rest.
Xereus, having been called forth so many times, tore a rift

1

between his daemonic plane and Fairelle, allowing thousands of daemons to pour into Pereum.

Years upon years of bloody warring went by with all races fighting for control and eventually the daemons gained dominion of the heart of Fairelle. Realizing that all lands would soon fall into the daemons' control, the High Elders of the Fae and the Mages from the south, combined their magicks to seal the rift. The daemons were banished back to their own plane, but Pereum was wiped off the map in the process, leaving only charred waste behind forever known as The Daemon Wastelands.

Upon the day of the rift closing, a Mage soothsayer prophesied of the healing of Fairelle. Over the next thousand years the races continued to war against each other, waiting for the day when the ancient prophesies would begin.

Eight prophesies, a thousand years old, to unite the lands and heal Fairelle. Now the Jätte will be found and possibly turn the tide of the war.

CHAPTER ONE

SOUTHEASTERN COAST, FAIRELLE - LATE FALL 1213 A.D. (AFTER DAEMONS)

"Y ou what?" Jak shouted.

"It's for your own good." Her father swayed and caught himself on a chair, barely capable of holding itself together.

"More likely it was for *your* own good. How is me being sold in a game of cards for my own good?" Jak slammed her fists on the rickety kitchen table, shaking it.

Her father straightened his drunken shoulders. "Jakleen don't you take a tone with me-"

She stepped closer to her father, making him back up. For all of his bluster she knew the truth, she terrified him.

"I'll take any tone I want. I am a person, not a horse, not a pig, not a chair. You cannot use me as a prize in a game of cards." She clenched her fists until her biceps shook. Her magic awoke in her veins, begging to be unleashed. "I will not marry that overbearing, brainless dolt, Rupert."

"You will! Because I am your father and I say you will."

3

She narrowed her gaze. "Oh, you think so, do you?"

Her father's gaze flicked to the side and he licked his lips before smiling. "Rupert is popular in the village and in the last few years he has become wealthier than anyone else. He will make you a decent husband and me a respectable son in law." He clumsily reached into his pocket and pulled something out. "And he gave me this for you." Her father held out a beautiful purple and pink-jeweled butterfly hairpin.

Jak took the pin and turned it over in her hand before throwing it at her father. "Where did he suddenly get all of this wealth? Did you even bother to ask? Stealing most likely."

"You don't know that." Her father burped and grabbed the poor wobbly chair with both hands.

"And what did he promise you if you let him marry me?"

Her father straightened and pushed back his shoulders. "He promised to be a suitable husband and provider and-"

Rage flowed through Jak. She grabbed a butter knife off the table and brandished it at her father.

"All right. He... he promised to pay all my debts in town and give me a small monthly allowance."

There it was. Just as she'd said. Her father had sold her for ale and card money. Jak threw the knife across the small house where it stuck in the wall just above her father's bed.

Her father screeched and ducked. "It was either that or sell your beloved cow, Annabelle."

"I or the cow, and you chose to keep the cow. Typical."

Her father had always been a wrung above swine snot but this... this was worse. How in the world could her mother have thought she'd be better off raised by him than with her in the forest?

Jak grabbed her thin jade green shawl and wrapped it around her shoulders. She pushed passed her father, sending him sprawling on his backside. He grumbled and cursed at her as she stepped out into the late summer morning.

The sun peeked over the hills as if checking to make sure everything was all clear. She kicked down the dirt path around the side of her house toward the rear. The chickens hadn't even left their nests yet and Annabelle's eyes still drooped. She shuffled to the animal and rubbed her creamy colored head.

"Sell the cow or his daughter. Not get a job so he can pay his debts. Makes perfect sense. He sees us as equals."

Annabelle continued to sleep as Jak kissed her warm head and then turned toward the road.

She spent the half mile trek into town trying to formulate a plan for getting herself out of the crap her father had gotten her into. Not that he'd done more than give his consent, which mattered very little to Jak. It was her decision that mattered most and she would be once again forced to let Rupert know in no uncertain terms that she had no interest in becoming his bride. Why couldn't he just get it through his lugheaded skull that she wanted nothing to do with him?

Two women eyed her as they milked cows and sorted the washing for the day. Jak pulled her shawl tighter around her shoulders giving herself as much courage as possible. The scent of yeast and rising bread made her stomach growl as she passed the bakery. She dug her nose into her shawl and imagined that she could smell her mother's scent on it, even though it had faded over a decade previous. She had enough money in her pocket to buy a loaf of bread, but she needed to save the money now more than ever. She might need it to get away. For the last ten years or more she had begun taking small amounts of money from her father when he won and keeping it in a pouch that she never removed from under her skirt. She had almost enough to start somewhere new, but with the most recent turn of events, she might have to leave sooner.

The fruits and vegetables she sold to the locals may be the best crop of anyone within a night's ride, but that didn't mean the townspeople paid her what her wares were worth. Everyone seemed pretty sure that she'd sacrificed newborn babies to the old gods to grow such great produce. But the truth was, she knew what plants needed to grow and took the time to care for them.

Jak stopped in front of the Ugly Ogre tavern and stared at the shamble of a building that resembled its name all too closely. She had expected it to fall down years prior, but the owner just kept fixing holes and shoring up places with new pieces of wood to keep it standing. Shoving open the creaky, weathered door the scent of stale alcohol and too many bodies slapped her with force. Her nose twitched as she looked around the mostly barren bar.

The pudgy owner, who resembled the name of his tavern as much as the building did, rubbed down the bar with a moth-ridden cloth. He stopped when he spotted her, but Jak paid him no mind. A bark of laughter flowed from the back room making Jak shudder in disgust. She squared her shoulders and headed for the sound.

"Miss," the owner called. "Miss, you can't go in there."

Another feeble attempt by a man to keep her in what *he* considered her place. But she knew the men of this town all too well. Not a one possessed the stones to stand up to her.

Jak pushed through the curtain separating the rooms and the three men lounging around the table glanced up from their cards. The two town rowdies' eyes widened at the sight of her, but Rupert smiled from beneath his perfectly shaped mustache.

"Hello, darling."

"Don't you dare call me that." She spat on the floor, making his smile crack for a moment.

"Why? We are engaged now, after all." He chuckled.

The two rowdies laid their cards on the table and leisurely bee-lined for the exit, keeping a full birth as they rounded her.

"How could you?" She took a step closer to him.

Rupert plopped his heavy booted foot on the table. "How could I what, darling?"

The word grated on her ears like a chisel. She clenched her fists trying to control her anger.

"I told you I wouldn't marry you last week, and the month before, and the month before that. How could you take a bet from my father for my hand in marriage knowing I despise you?"

"Take it from him? Darling, I'm the one who suggested the deal."

Fury pulsed through her so hard she could barely see his smug expression any longer.

"Jakleen. Why are you fighting this? I will build you the grandest house in town. Furnish it with beautiful things and lavish you with anything you want. In return, you will adore and love me and give me children aplenty. Why is this a bad thing? No one else will take you."

"If it's adoration you want, let me show you the adoration I have in store for you."

With a flick of her wrist the floorboards creaked and groaned underneath his chair. Tree roots burst through the planks knocking him backward. She pushed the roots at him and squeezed them around his body until he squealed like a terrified piglet. What a coward. She didn't squeeze enough to hurt him, only enough for him to realize he would never control her. She would never be his.

Wide-eyed, Rupert pleaded for help like a little girl, making Jak shake her head. He struggled against the thick roots, but they didn't budge. Jak sauntered to him, the feel of the roots as much a part of her as if she held him in the palm of her hand.

"I will never marry you, Rupert. I will never love you. I will never adore you. If you try to force me into marriage, I can assure you, you are going to spend a lot of time pinned to the floor. And not in a way you will enjoy."

She pulled her loose shawl back around her shoulders and stormed out of the room to the sounds of Rupert's continued screams. She stepped into the bar area where the two thugs as well as the tavern owner stared at her. Jak eyed each of them in turn, but none of them said a word, so she headed to the exit.

Heavy footsteps ran to the back room behind her.

"My toth, look what she did!"

"Get an axe, you dolts!" Rupert yelled.

Jak stepped out onto the dirt street and scanned both ways. People exited their houses at the sounds of Rupert's distress.

She huffed down the front step of the tavern, the wind mixing with Rupert's screams. People drew closer to the tavern, being sure to give her a wide birth.

"Holy mother! The old willow," a woman cried.

Jak rounded the corner, and sure enough, the ancient willow leaned over the top of the tavern like an ominous giant hand. Its roots spread underneath the structure.

"An axe," someone yelled from behind her. "We need an axe!"

Jak's anger abated at the thought that they would chop up a friend that had come to her aid. Jak moved to the tree and laid her hand on its trunk.

"Thank you, my friend," she whispered.

She caressed the soft bark and bid the tree to release Rupert. The tree groaned and retreated. Its roots slid out from under the tavern making the entire building shake. When the tree settled, she touched it again, lending her strength and comfort. Jak peered up into the swaying branches, though no breeze blew.

"Slumber and dream. Drink and grow."

The tree hummed with energy and several new buds popped open high in the foliage.

Rupert's voice echoed through the tavern and he burst through the front door with a bang.

"Where the hell is she?" he demanded. "Where is Jakleen?"

Jak shook her head and sighed. The man really must not have a brain if he thought confronting her was wise.

She stepped out into the street and waited for him to notice her. He turned in a circle looking from face to face of the gathered crowd. Finally, his gaze landed on her.

"You." He pointed at her.

"I'm me."

"You tried to kill me. She made that tree move and tried to kill me with it. She's a witch."

Jak laughed. "I'd like to see a witch with as much magick in her entire reliquary as I have in the palm of one hand. Want me to show you?"

Jak smirked as everyone quickly vacated the street- including Rupert.

CHAPTER TWO

T he king sucked in a raspy, shallow breath. Stefan mopped his brow with a cool wet rag and swallowed hard. This wasn't happening. His father was not dying.

"We need to retaliate," said his younger brother Ivan. "The stalk will be back tonight. We should go down there and—"

"No," replied Stefan. "Father wouldn't want that."

"I am sure father would not want to be laying in his bed dying because a stupid human got greedy and wanted mother's jewels, either."

Stefan gritted his teeth and continued to wipe down his father. For nearly a year a human male had been sneaking up the beanstalk and stealing from them. Little things at first. A golden egg and a silver goblet, then a jeweled necklace. All small stuff. Things his father said they could do without, though they could've been used to procure well-needed supplies for the kingdom. But in the past three months the items had gotten larger, and there had been more of them taken. A golden harp was stolen two months past, though Stefan had no idea how the man had even gotten down the beanstalk with it.

But this last month he'd tried to steal Stefan's father, King Julius's crown from his father's room, while he slept. His father had awoken, and the human had stabbed his father low in the abdomen. It should've healed within a few days, but it hadn't, and now the infection spread like a brushfire and Stefan was out of ideas.

"We should go down," said Ivan. "We should at least go and try to find some medicine or a healer."

"And what? Ask them nicely to please come up to the Jätte kingdom in the clouds and stay as our guest for a few weeks to help father? That we promise we will return them safely? Do you honestly think such a thing will work?"

Ivan scooted from his heavy wooden chair tipping it backward. "It's better than sitting here doing nothing."

Stefan turned his gaze to his younger brother. Though Stefan stood close to ten feet tall and Ivan was a head shorter, Ivan had at least fifty pounds on him. So, in a fight they were evenly matched.

"Is that what you think I've been doing here for the last weeks? That tending to father has been nothing? Searching the library for answers has been nothing? Making poultices out of what little we have left in the infirmary is nothing!"

Stefan's father coughed, and his glassy, grey eyes turned toward him as he reached for Stefan's hand.

"Do not fight my sons," their father breathed. "What is done is done. Soon... Soon I fear I shall leave you and it will be up to you, Stefan, to keep our people going."

"Our people?" said Ivan. "Father, our women left for other kingdoms years ago. How is Stefan going to save our people?"

Julius' gaze turned to Ivan. "You've always been strong in spirit, Ivan, like your mother. But to bring our people back to greatness you must also possess a level head, like your brother Stefan. Strength without the wisdom is worthless."

Their father hacked, and blood trickled from the corner of his mouth. Stefan wiped his father's lips and picked up a cup of tea, holding it for Julius to sip.

"Drink," said Stefan. "We will find a way to fix this. You will come back to us, stronger than ever."

Ivan shook his shaggy pearl colored head.

"I need a drink." Ivan's storm colored eyes brewed with frustration as he stomped out. His heavy footsteps clomped down the hallway as he headed down to the great hall. So much like their mother. Stalky, light haired, light eyed, light skinned, but with a temper as dark as Mount Hurluck at the edge of the Cloudlands.

Though Stefan could understand Ivan's frustration. They were down to fewer than one hundred Jätte left in their kingdom, and with no women, their country would be dead within a generation.

Something needed to be done. But that was a problem for another day. The issue at hand remained—how did

Stefan keep his kingdom from losing just one man. His father.

Jak spent the day in the woods, knowing if she went home, she might kill her father. By noon her legs were in need of a rest, and she headed toward a small cottage occupied by a young fae woman. Jak hadn't taken to prying about the girl's past and why she'd traveled so far from home, but the two had become friends, and Jak stopped by every once and a while to spend an afternoon with Olivia.

She strolled through the trees and into a small alcove near a hefty cliff. At the base of it, mostly hidden in the shade of the mountain, was the small wooden cabin, a light curl of smoke wafting from the chimney. Jak hiked toward the entrance between two sizeable vegetable beds. In them most every plant waned in the lack of sunlight. It surprised Jak that Olivia was unable to use her magick to make the vegetables and fruits grow; after all, the fae were known for their excellent produce. But perhaps Olivia didn't know how to use such magick.

Off to the right of the cabin Olivia had also set up a small training ground of sorts. Wooden dummies stood, battered and beaten. A series of targets hung on various trees up to fifty yards away, riddled with holes from both arrows as well as knives. A javelin even stuck out of a target near the end. Jak wondered what kind of war Olivia was waiting for. Or worse, what kind of war she'd already been through.

The scent of soup floated by, making Jak's stomach growl. Light humming floated out from inside the cabin. Jak stepped up to the cracked and worn door. She listened for a moment to the beautiful melody while noticing the large pile of stacked, chopped firewood. An axe stuck in a stump and Jak wondered how long it had taken Olivia to chop it all. She wasn't by any means a burly girl, far from it, yet she seemed to possess great strength, or maybe it was sheer determination, Jak wasn't sure which.

She knocked on the door. "Olivia? It's Jak."

The humming stopped and light footsteps strode to the door. It swung open and Olivia smiled.

"Well hello." Olivia looked Jak up and down. "What's wrong? Why are you in your night clothes?"

Jak shook her head.

"Come in. Sit down. You don't even have shoes on."

Jak entered the small hut, realizing for the first time how cold she'd become. The fire warmed her immediately making her realize how chilly the day had been outside. She sat on a small rickety chair and peered down at her feet.

"Oh, I am so sorry. I'm getting mud all over your floor."

Olivia laughed. "I get mud on it every day. But here, let me help you warm up."

Olivia pushed Jak's chair nearer to the fire and wrapped a bulky tattered blanket around her.

"Would you like some soup? I was just about to have some."

Jak nodded. "Thank you."

Olivia pushed the table closer to the fire as Jak stared

into the flames. She poured soup for Jak and herself, and then produced a crude loaf of bread and some butter.

"I'm so sorry. I didn't bring you any milk, either."

"Pish tosh." Olivia waved her hand. "Though I will never turn down a jug of fresh milk and cream, it is not at all why I like you. You never owe me anything, Jak, you know that."

Jak looked around. Olivia's hut was in worse shape than even Jak's cabin, and that said a lot. Even so, it was devoid of any personal items. There were no trinkets or heirlooms left to her by family. No portraits of loved ones or the place she'd left behind. Nothing but a wall of various weapons, a tattered, once colorful quilt that looked like it had been discarded years previous, and a roughly carved chest with a lock on it.

"Olivia, why don't you come with me to town? Stay with me instead of out here by yourself?" Jak asked for the dozenth time.

Olivia shook her head. "I've not yet found a town in Fairelle amenable to my… differences."

Jak gave her a sad smile. She knew all too well the feeling of being different. With her bright blue eyes that matched her hair perfectly, she tended to stick out anywhere she went. "Mayhaps we will find one together."

Olivia's expression brightened and her beautiful doe eyes crinkled in the corners. "I'd like that."

Jak's gaze pulled to the large chest again. Curiosity threatened to get the better of her and make her ask Olivia what was so valuable that she kept it in a locked trunk in a cabin at the edge of a mountain where no one was likely to find her—but she didn't.

Jak sipped the bland soup and reminded herself she needed to bring Olivia some herb seeds the next time she came.

"So, what happened?" Olivia stirred her soup and Jak noticed a bandage on her hand for the first time.

"What happened to you?" Jak pointed at the wrapping.

"Oh. It's nothing. I was practicing my throwing skills and my palm slipped down the blade."

"I can look at it if you'd like."

Olivia shook her head. "It's not too bad. Besides, you aren't getting out of your story that easily."

Shame melted into her stomach at once again having to tell someone about something her father had done.

"I do not understand why my mother would give me to a man such as my father."

They sat in silence for several moments as they ate. That was one thing Jak appreciated about Olivia, she knew when to speak and when silence was a better option.

"For that matter I cannot understand why my mother slept with a man such as my father to produce a child."

Again, Olivia said nothing for a long moment.

"I often wonder what my father saw in my mother," she finally said. "My father was an honest, kind man and my mother never bore anything but selfishness and vindictiveness."

"Toward you?"

Olivia regarded her soup bowl. "In her way, yes, to me as well, but more to my half-sister, Cinder."

Sadness drooped Olivia's features.

Jak's attention peaked. She'd never once heard Olivia speak of her family. "Is your family still living?"

Olivia looked up. "My sister is, but not my parents."

"Do you miss them?"

Olivia took several long, slow spoonfuls of soup and Jak wasn't sure if she would answer the question. Had she over-stepped?

"I miss my father. Not so much my mother. Though there are a great many things I wish I could ask her. Things I don't understand about who I am. I miss my sister the most, though."

"Do you not see her?"

Olivia stirred her soup and then broke off a piece of bread and handed it to Jak. "What about you? Why are you out in the woods in your night clothes?" Olivia's abrupt smile and change of subject told Jak she'd finished sharing for the day.

"My father sold me to be married."

"What?" The shock on Olivia's face mimicked Jak's own.

"I couldn't believe it either. He sold me off like an ox cart. Rupert agreed to pay off all of his debts and give him a monthly stipend for my hand. My father agreed."

"You aren't going through with it, are you?"

Jak chuckled. "You want an extended house guest?"

"I wouldn't mind if you stayed. Though I don't think you would enjoy being here after a while. This life seems a bit too solitary for you. But I could at least feed you. And I promise not to sell you to anyone."

Jak chuckled. The thought appealed to her for a

moment. No people staring or gawking as she walked by. No mothers whispering and pulling their children away. No men snickering. Best of all, no father to take care of and make sure he didn't drink himself to death.

Jak sighed and swallowed another spoonful of soup. As much as she would love to be rid of it all, she couldn't just walk away. Her mother had left her there for a reason, and she needed to discover why. No matter what it took.

THE SUN DIPPED LOW BEHIND THE TREES WHEN JAK PEEKED out the window of Olivia's hut. She'd spent the entire day talking and helping Olivia, drying meat and preserving berries found in the forest, collecting roots and plants for healing. Jak loved her time with Olivia, but the longer she stayed, the more sadness seeped into her bones making her skin itch with the need to leave. As if the longer she remained the more acutely aware she became that this forest was not her home. Her heart belonged somewhere else. Somewhere she had not yet found.

"It's getting late."

Olivia glanced out the window. "You could stay the night if you'd like."

Jak smiled. "Thank you. I appreciate your offer. Your friendship means more than you know. But I must get going."

"What do you think will happen when you get back? Do you think Rupert will insist you marry him?"

"Not if he knows what's good for him."

Olivia laughed and nodded. "You are so much like my sister." Pain tinged her voice, despite the smile on her lips.

Jak hugged Olivia tight. "I'll come back soon. And you know where I am if you ever need anything."

Olivia nodded. "I'll always keep the kettle on for you."

Jak picked up her shawl and wrapped it around her shoulders. She headed out and stopped. Olivia brushed her hair behind her ear, revealing the pointy tips belying her Fae heritage. Jak wondered for the millionth time if she shouldn't try to reach out somehow and find Olivia's sister. But it wasn't her place. If Olivia wanted her sister to know where she was, she would've contacted her herself.

A boom crashed through the forest, and both of them turned toward the window.

"Sounds like thunder," said Olivia. "I should get the buckets out for the leaks in case it rains." She pulled several battered pots and pans from a cabinet and began setting them around the room.

"Would you like some help?"

"No, no. I'm well acquainted with each of the six leaks. You should get going, though, before you get soaked."

Jak hated the thought of Olivia being alone in a wet hut, but her friend had been doing so for at least two years.

Jak opened the door and sniffed the air. There was no moisture to be tasted. If rain were coming, it wouldn't be that night.

She walked down the walkway and stopped near the garden beds. The plants stared at her accusingly. Olivia's friendship helped her more than Jak could say.

"All right," she muttered. "But if Olivia gets mad at me

for helping, it's your fault, so you better produce twice as much."

Jak walked to one of the beds and dug her fingers into the soil. She breathed deep and felt for the roots of each life. She pushed her request out through the ground and strengthened the roots. She pushed nutrients and water into the plants. Gradually, they began to straighten. The blossoms unfolded, and the vegetables and fruits emerged, vibrant and healthy. Jak smiled and knelt by the other bed. A hissing whisper caught her attention, and she looked around. In the dimming light, she couldn't see very far into the trees. No branch creaked, no leaves rustled, nothing. She knelt down in front of the second bed and dug her fingers into the dirt. Again, the plants grew tall and strong, laden with fruit and vegetables. She stood and picked a ripe strawberry, popping it into her mouth. Perfect.

Jak hurried away from the hut and wound her way through the trees without thinking. She headed toward town, allowing her feet to carry her. She'd gone several hundred yards when again a hushed whisper floated toward her. Jak spun on the spot looking into the looming darkness.

"Who's there?" she called.

No reply.

She searched the ground for something to arm herself with. "Rupert, if you think you can get the upper hand on me, think again. I'm in a forest, surrounded by trees, you've witnessed twice today what I can do."

A tree groaned several feet away. Jak spun toward it and peered into the blackness beyond.

"If you think you can sneak up on me, you are sorely mistaken."

Only the sound of Jak's heartbeat echoed. She unfurled her arms and reached out to the trees surrounding her. Vines ripped from the bark and floated toward her. She waited as minutes ticked by, and the whispers started again. She couldn't make out the words, but she could hear at least two distinct voices arguing. Two of them. She wasn't sure she could take on two. Her heart thundered and the hairs on her body stood on end as the trees whispered a warning to her. Without waiting another moment, Jak turned and fled.

The sounds of a dozen thuds bumped the soft ground as the vines fell to the forest floor. She sent a silent apology to the trees for having not put them back the way she'd found them.

"Get her!" a deep voice yelled.

The ground shook as the men rushed after her. Trees around her trembled and quaked. Her head told her to look at who chased her, but her heart couldn't bear to see.

She whipped through the trees; the moonlight flashed up ahead. She still had quite a ways to go before anyone would hear her cries for help—not that they'd help anyway. Not after what had happened in town earlier.

Jak rushed past a Ubling tree, and it grabbed at her clothes. She dropped her shawl and continued forward. Closer, closer. Suddenly a warm mass pressed into her back, shoving her to the ground.

"I got her!" A deep voice bellowed.

"Don't let her go," another voice yelled from afar.

Jak struggled underneath the weight of the huge figure. "Get off me! Get off!" she screeched.

Reaching down through the ground she pulled roots from their resting places and wrapped them around the enormous body. The man yanked against them, breaking them with his powerful legs.

"Stop that," he shouted.

"Stop smothering me," she replied.

"She's tanglin' me up!" he called.

Jak breathed harder as she pulled more and more roots from the ground, wrapping them around the man's legs and torso, but with every root she pulled, he fought, breaking it apart.

"All right, enough." Two gigantic hands pulled her from under the first man and lifted her off the ground. The pale man towering over her shook her like a rag doll. "Stop."

"Let go of me." Jak swung at him and missed. She swung again and connected with something soft.

"Dammit!"

"Let her go, she's not worth it," said the other getting to his feet.

"She can help my father."

"I'm not helping you, you big oaf! I'd never help you after the way you manhandled me."

He pulled her close, his face looming over her. For a split second, her blood froze. His head loomed larger than any man she'd ever encountered. Thick, long braided creamy hair hung over his shoulders and tickled her bare skin. Deep-set grey eyes stared at her from under a heavy brow.

"You will help my father, or you will die."

Terror gave way to fury as Jak offered a silent apology to the forest and pulled with all her strength. A tall Fenlen tree next to her groaned and the ground trembled in pain as the tree uprooted and fell sideways.

"Look out!" the first man yelled.

The man holding her dropped her to the ground as the giant tree toppled over. She hadn't realized how far off the ground she had been. She rolled several times as he caught the tree and strained against the weight of it.

Jak scrambled backward only to be picked up by the first man. She hardly noticed, being unable to take her eyes from the falling tree. A gut gripping ache made her breath shudder at the realization of what she'd done. Yes, trees died over time. They fell, they broke, they became diseased, but she bore the fault alone for this death. Sadness and guilt crept in, threatening to overwhelm her.

"Put her down and help me, dammit!" The man yelled.

The first man dropped her to the ground with a thud. She fell back, and her head cracked on a thick root. The trees spun and the moon swayed in and out of view. The cries of the toppled tree grew fainter in her veins like the slowing of a heartbeat.

The men pushed at the tree trunk, trying to keep it from squashing them. Jak reached out with a shaky hand and called it. Its life force already almost entirely gone. Jak pushed with her strength and appealed to other trees and vines for help in righting her wrong. The other trees reached with vines and branches and roots, taking hold of their fallen sibling and straining to pull it upright once more. The effort shook Jak's entire body, but inch-by-inch the tree righted itself, crashing back into place.

Jak sucked in a deep breath, stretched out both hands pushing the tree roots back into the ground; deep into the fertile soil.

"I'm sorry," Jak whispered. "I'm so sorry."

The forest fell silent as she lay crumpled on the ground. She stared up at the trees, feeling their shock and fear flow through her.

She dug her fingers into the ground. "I'm sorry," she whispered again.

The men loomed over her. "Yeah, we're sorry too."

The leader picked her up like a child. She shivered in the night air from fatigue and chill.

"Put me down." Her voice came out weaker than she'd meant for it to.

"Sorry," said the man. "Not until you heal my father."

He hefted her over his shoulder like a sack of potatoes. Jak could scarcely move from exhaustion. From over his shoulder, she glimpsed the man behind him as they hit a patch of clearing and the moon shone down. He wasn't as pale as her captor. His skin carried more of an ashy grey color and his eyes were so dark she couldn't see them at all. But strangest of all was his hair. The mossy green color was the first she'd ever seen that came anywhere close to the color of her own hair.

Minutes passed and she caught the scent of smoke as they passed Olivia's cabin about thirty yards away. She wanted to yell out for help, but she didn't want to put Olivia in any danger. The men stopped at the edge of the tall mountain cliff and then the man holding her grabbed something with both hands.

"Hang on to me," he said.

Then suddenly, the ground grew further and further away as they climbed higher and higher.

Terror mixed with fascination until the air grew thinner and the leafy forest floor disappeared. Jak fought to keep her eyes open until she couldn't anymore, and everything went black.

CHAPTER THREE

"What the *hell* did you do?" Stefan grabbed Ivan by the throat and slammed him into the wall, making the room shake.

Ivan fought unsuccessfully to pry Stefan's hand from his throat. "I'm doing whatever it takes."

Anger bubbled inside Stefan so hot he thought his head might explode.

"A woman. You kidnapped a human woman from the world below. Who the hell does that?"

Ivan shoved Stefan in the chest, forcing him back. "The kind of man who wants to save his father's life."

"And you think I don't?"

Ivan stepped forward invading Stefan's space. "I think you're too much like father. Too soft to do what is required."

Stefan rammed his finger into brother's chest. "And you are too much like mother. Hotheaded, aggressive and impulsive."

"Perhaps if father had been a bit more like that our lands wouldn't be barren and our men starving."

Ivan was wrong. Their mother left because of her arrogance and pride. Being the strongest in the room or the most aggressive wasn't always the way to win an argument. Their father wanted to get along with humans, not pillage and raid and destroy. But their mother had been raised in a different kingdom where there was no such thing as trying to get along with the humans. To her it was nothing more than weakness. So, she'd taken what few women and female children remained in the kingdom and left.

Stefan stared at his brother for a long minute, sure that if he opened his mouth, it would end with the two of them coming to blows.

"While father is ill, I am in charge of the kingdom," said Stefan. "And I told you not to go down there. You are confined to your chambers until I decide otherwise."

"I tried to do what you wouldn't. Save him."

Stefan stepped ever closer to Ivan, looming over him. "If you fight me, I will win. Either way, you will end up in your chambers. Whether it be shackled or whether it be loose 'tis up to you."

Ivan's fists clenched and unclenched several times. Finally, he turned and strode from the room, curses, and profanity following him all the way out. Stefan didn't move for several minutes as he fought to keep from slamming his fist into the wall. He couldn't believe what Ivan had done. And now with the beanstalk gone for a fortnight, they had no way of putting the woman back on the ground.

He glanced around his large bedroom toward the door

on the far wall that adjoined her chamber to his. He had no idea what to expect. He hadn't even asked Ivan why he'd taken that particular woman. All he knew was that there was a tiny, frightened female in the next room, and he needed to do his best to try and make her as comfortable as possible until the next beanstalk cycle.

Stefan ran his fingers through his thick dark hair and looked down at his clothes. They weren't his finest things. His cream tunic was clean, though it bore a hole in one elbow and his brown breeches were thin, but hadn't worn through at the knees yet. His boots could use a polishing, but they too were not in bad shape. All things considered, it was as good as it was going to get, considering there were no women to help mend the clothes and there were no men who sewed.

Stefan stepped up to the adjoining wooden door and listened to the room beyond. Not a peep emanated. It was possible she still slept, but something told him she wasn't sleeping, after the yelling match between him and Ivan.

He knocked softly before grasping the handle and opened the door a crack. He scanned the room, but there was no one there.

"Hello? I'm Stefan and—"

A pitcher hurled his way. Stefan shut the door just in time to miss being hit in the head. It crashed against the wooden surface and shattered.

"Please. I know you must be angry and confused, but—"

"Angry? You don't know the meaning of the word," came a small, feisty voice from the other room.

He opened the door again. "If you'll let me explain—"

For a flash of a second, he spotted a slender woman in what appeared to be a nightgown near the bed before the dish that accompanied the pitcher hurdled at him as well.

"Please," he begged. "I'm sure this is very upsetting."

"You think this is very upsetting?" In rapid succession, several more pieces of China beat against the door.

Damn Ivan and damn his stupidity.

Stefan took a deep breath and yanked the door wide. "Now look!"

A stone statue of a horse flew toward him. He grabbed it before it could hit him in the chest and set it on a table. "I actually like that statue."

In front of him stood the most beautiful, diminutive woman he'd ever seen. Long, aquamarine hair hung down to her waist. Round seafoam blue eyes looked up at him from behind thick dark lashes. Every inch that he could see of her slender, pale body held a delicate air. But for all of her slenderness, her throwing arm was decent and her aim spot on. She scanned him up and down and then grabbed the oversized standing candelabra off the floor and wielded it in front of her.

"You know you are amazingly strong for a human of your size."

She stabbed at him with the metal stand.

"I am strong, so you better stay away from me."

Stefan threw his hands in the air and kept himself from smiling. She was spunky, he liked that.

"I don't want to hurt you."

"Like the man who grabbed me and threw me over his

shoulder? Or the other one who tackled and pinned me down?"

Anger rumbled in Stefan's chest. "That was uncalled for, and punishment will be dealt out to Galin, the one who tackled you, I promise. As for my brother Ivan. He took you because—"

"Brother? How fitting. I'm aware of why he took me. Something about fixing your father. Well, I'm sorry. I cannot help you. And I refuse to be held prisoner any longer, so let me go!"

She lobbed the candelabra at him, and Stefan caught it a split second before it smashed him in the shoulder.

"I like this piece too." He set the candelabra down and took a breath before looking back at her again—but she'd disappeared. He scanned the room as he advanced, crunching on the broken pottery.

"I don't want to hurt you, trust me, and I want nothing more than to get you back to the ground and your people, but there is a bit of a problem. You see, the beanstalk Ivan carried you up won't be back for a fortnight. So, unfortunately, you must stay here until it does. Not as a prisoner I assure you, but as a guest. My guest."

He stopped at the foot of the bed, but she didn't emerge. She was quick, he'd give her that. He peered on either side before spotting the wardrobe. He walked to it and pulled the doors open gingerly.

"I promise I don't want to hurt you."

No female.

He opened the closet, but she wasn't there either. She

wasn't that tiny. She had to be somewhere. A slight breeze ruffled his hair, and he turned. *Oh no.*

Stefan ran to the small window and leaned out. The woman hung on the castle wall, hugging the vines that grew up above the window.

"Be careful," he shouted. "You'll fall."

"I am an excellent climber." She stretched out her fingers, and a vine reached toward her, wrapping around her wrists and pulling her upward.

"My grandfather's beard," Stefan exclaimed. "How did you do that?"

"Stay away." She reached up and dug her fingers into a crack between the stones.

"Please come back inside before you get hurt." Stefan tried to squeeze through the small window. He couldn't just run through the castle to the outside. By the time he got up to the roof and shimmied down that side she'd have fallen for sure. He got one shoulder out but several jagged shards of stone bit into his other shoulder as he tried to squeeze further out. *Dammit.*

"Please," Stefan begged. "The ground on this side of the castle tends to give way if tread upon and falling back to the low ground is not likely the way you want to get there. Though it would be quicker, I suppose."

"Quicker than what?"

"Then waiting for the beanstalk to return. As I tried to explain it, only comes once every fortnight. That is the only way to get you back to your people."

"Two weeks?"

"Like I said, falling to the low ground is quicker. And

even if you do manage to get away from this castle, I assure you the other Jätte kingdoms will not be quite so welcoming as I am offering to be."

She scrunched up her face and swore the likes of which would make even Ivan blush. Her brightly colored hair whipped around her face in the stiff breeze. The vines holding her groaned.

Stefan waited a moment and then extended his hand to her. "I'm Prince Stefan of Luften."

She stared at his hand and he prayed she would take it so he could pull her to safety. She licked her lips and eyed the top of the castle as if gauging whether or not she could make it. She glanced down momentarily again hugging the wall with her whole body.

Great! She was afraid of heights.

He needed to get her inside before her fear overtook her and she found herself the victim of unfortunate circumstances.

"Please don't chance it. I can see this is not what you want to be doing. Come inside, and we can talk this over."

There were several snaps in rapid succession as the vines that she'd been holding onto broke free of the stone. She screamed and fell several inches.

"Give me your hand!"

She tried to grab onto the vines, but with every fistful she touched they broke from the wall. Stefan watched helplessly as she frantically tried to climb upward, speaking to the vines in words he couldn't make out. But for whatever reason, the vines no longer wrapped around her as they had previously. As if they'd changed their minds and left her to fend for herself.

"Come down," he called. "Please. Let me help you."

"I can't," she replied.

"Reach with your feet then bring down your hands."

It was too late. The vines broke free and she tumbled from their grasp. She screamed as she rushed closer to Stefan. He stretched as far as he could and he wrapped his hand around her upper arm. She screeched and clawed at him. Stefan strained against the stone that threatened to break his shoulder if he pressed on it any harder and drew her toward the castle. Her small hands landed on the windowsill, and he helped her inside.

She set her dirty feet on the stone floor, and he stepped away from her as she leaned heavily on the wall, shaking. Stefan waited, afraid she might try and climb out again if he scared her. After several moments she stood up straight and brushed leaves and dirt from her nightgown. When she finished, she regarded him with her sparkling, tear-streaked eyes. Her cheeks flushed a deep rose color from the strong winds, and her hair stood up all over in a tangled mess. All in all, she was damn lucky that messy hair and pink cheeks was all she'd gotten out of the ordeal. He hated to think what would have happened if he hadn't caught her.

"Uh... You have a vine in your hair," Stefan finally said.

She reached up and patted the top of her head, missing it. Stefan stepped closer and reached toward her, but she moved back a step and continued to pat her head. After a minute he finally reached over and plucked the vine from her hair.

She barely came up to his torso she was so small. And the way he'd wrapped his hand around her arm made her seem impossibly fragile, though he was sure she was anything but.

He stepped back, but she caught his sleeve.

"You're bleeding."

He looked down at his shoulder that still ached from being pressed into the window. "It's nothing."

"But…" She stopped before her fingers touched his skin and pulled back a pace. "You should wash that before infection sets in."

Stefan tried to cover the skin with his now ripped tunic. He was quickly running out of presentable clothing.

"I've never seen anything like what you did out there. It was as if the vines were helping you at first," he said.

"They were. But their language is a bit different here than on the ground, so I am not sure they understood what I wanted."

"You speak to plants?"

"I'm a dryad. Trees and vines run in my blood. Just ask your brother about the tree I felled on his head."

"You uprooted a tree on Ivan?"

"He deserved it. Though I must say, the poor tree did not."

Stefan couldn't help but burst into laughter.

"What's so funny?" she demanded.

"You felt bad for the tree instead of Ivan." He continued to laugh. "I don't blame you."

"The tree did nothing to me. Your brother on the other hand tried, and eventually succeeded in kidnapping me so yes, my feelings are with the trees and not your brother's head."

Stefan nodded. "Quite so. I'm impressed at your quick wit as to think of such a thing."

"Do you believe females to be inferior in intellect?"

Her straightforward manner set him on edge. "Uh... no... I simply meant not many people would have been that quick to think of something while being kidnapped."

A thick silence fell between them as if in a standoff.

"So, a dryad." he said.

She ran her fingers through her hair and began to braid part of it up. "Half dryad. My father is human."

"Is that why your hair is that color?"

She finished getting her hair out of her face and set her fists on her hips, regarding him. "How tall are you?"

"Almost ten feet. How tall are you?"

"So, you are a giant?"

"Low grounders call us giants. But our true name is Jätte."

"Jätte."

Stefan smiled. "Do you have a name?"

"Jakleen. But I prefer Jak."

"Jak. Interesting choice, but it suits you. I'm Stefan."

"Yes, you said. Prince Stefan of Luften."

She looked down and suddenly her cheeks flushed again and she covered her breasts with her arms. "Do you perhaps own something I might be able to change into? I am not quite comfortable wearing my nightgown in front of a stranger."

"But weren't you in the forest in your nightgown?"

"Yes but... that was different. I had a shawl, which I lost running from your brother, and I was in the woods because... because I just was."

"I'm not sure we have anything small enough for you, perhaps there is something left over from one of the girls. I'll see." Stefan turned to leave.

"Is that the exit," she pointed.

"Yes. Well, sort of. This room is attached to my room, and the only way in or out is through my room. I'll lock the door—"

"I refuse to be locked in."

"No, I'm not going to lock you in, but lock the others out. For your safety."

She cocked an eyebrow at him. "Isn't that the same thing? Locked is locked."

Stefan ran his hand through his long hair. "Well, why don't I leave this door unlocked and only lock the outer?"

She stared at him skeptically.

"You can always go out the window again if I don't come back for you. But mind the sharp shards on the floor. I'll sweep them up as soon as I return. And please don't break anything else. We don't have many nice things left here in Luften."

She nodded. "Why is there a bedroom that connects only to your bedroom and not a hallway?"

"It's for my wife. All Jätte prize their wives and children above anything else."

"So, you lock them away?"

"Our chamber systems are designed so that if the castle is attacked, invaders would not only be forced to go through all our defenses to get inside but once inside, they would need to go through every husband to get at the rooms holding the wives and children. The doors for the wives' rooms are made of the strongest iron and petrified wood we possess."

"And where is your wife?"

Stefan's chest tightened. "There are no wives in Luften."

"What, did you kidnap them as well and they escaped?"

Frustration tensed his shoulders. "They left of their freewill."

"So, you were married?"

"No. My father arranged a marriage for me with another kingdom, but when my mother and the other women left the engagement dissolved."

The painful memories squeezed in on his mind like a vise. Jak opened her mouth to no doubt ask another question but the weight of the memories forced Stefan to leave before she could ask. He flung open the outer door and closed it quickly. He then pulled the key from around his neck and locked the door. He set his head against the wood and blew out a breath as he pushed away the painful memories. Not of the one he'd been engaged to, but of watching his mother carry his little sisters out the gates of Luften.

He cleared his head and his mind turned to the beautiful, but tiny, dryad-human in his room. She'd been fierce, and intelligent, independent and quite inquisitive. He wasn't sure if he liked that about her- or if he couldn't stand it.

Jak watched Stefan hurry from the room. She waited for the door to close and then listened for the sound of the lock. She slumped to the floor and pulled her knees in tight. He was the most significant person she'd ever seen. His long, black braided hair had connected down his bluish-grey face with his dark sideburns. Thick black lashes had framed the bright green eyes that reminded her of summer grass. All in all, he was uniquely handsome, powerful and utterly terrifying.

She'd done what she always did. Put up a front and let him think she'd been brave when inside she'd been scared enough to stupidly go out the window. But he'd been gentle with her. Even when she'd thrown things at him and tried to impale him with the candelabra, he'd remained calm. And when she'd climbed out the window, he'd shown genuine concern for her wellbeing instead of anger. He hadn't yelled or threatened. He'd just tried to get her to come back inside. Whether that was because he still thought she could heal his father or not, she didn't know. She rubbed her arm, remembering the way his enormous, calloused hand had grasped it, saving her. She measured with her fingers to gauge how big his hand really was. It had wrapped around her so easily that as she fell, she'd feared he might rip it from her body. A sensation raced through her at the memory of his warm hand on her skin. A sensation she'd never felt before. Jak scowled and chastised herself for the feelings, shoving them away. This was no time to lose her head over a handsome... gigantic man.

She stared at her feet and tried to brush the dirt from them. Her communication with the vines had been strange.

She could feel them, but it had been as if they possessed only the most primitive of languages. Like children almost, and the more panicked she'd become, the more scared they'd become. The moment she'd accidentally broken one from the wall that had been the end. They'd no longer been willing to help her or communicate with her, and she'd fallen. For a moment, she'd thought she was going to die. Dropping through the air to the ground below, impaled on one of the trees in Olivia's forest. But he'd saved her. She doubted very highly his brother Ivan would've done the same.

After her heartbeat and shaking abated, Jak got to her feet and headed to the door, being careful not to step on any of what remained of her temper tantrum. She felt badly for having broken his items, but at the time, how could she have known he wouldn't grab her and gobble her up. That's what giants did, right? They ate humans like her? At least those were the legends.

She peered into the other vast bedroom and wove her way to the door. Walking amongst the oversized furniture made her feel like a child again. A bed befitting ten human men stood in one corner, sheets rumpled and unkempt. A tall, thin wardrobe stood slightly ajar next to the bed. A dark wooden table holding an oil lamp, along with an ornate desk and chair finished out the room. Jak took several steps toward the bed and found miscellaneous articles of clothing scattered around the floor. Without thinking she began to pick them up. The heavy worn fabric needed a thorough washing. She held up one of the tunics against her skin and caught Stefan's musky fragrance. Again, the strange sensation rolled through her belly. His shirt hung three times as wide as her shoulders and down past her knees in length. If they were any indication of the size of the clothing he might find for her to wear, she was going to need a belt—or three —to keep them on.

Jak did her best to fold them and then set them on the chair. She found herself laughing at how strange she felt being so small, but somehow the feeling of being surrounded by such large, heavy items comforted her. Like being in the forest amongst her friends, the ever-growing trees.

She busied herself by climbing up on the bed and straightening it as well. As much as she hated cleaning, it had been the thing she'd done to occupy her mind and body when waiting for her father to come home from the tavern. Or after an argument with him about his drinking. Or when she'd run out of books to read and had nothing better to do. It was more habit than enjoyment.

A knock sounded on the door and then a key turned in the lock. Jak hid behind the bed as Stefan entered carrying a tan dress made of animal skins. He closed the door and glanced about the room, spotting her.

"It belonged to... a young girl. It should fit you somewhat."

"Thank you." Jak didn't leave her spot.

Stefan surveyed the room. "You didn't need to clean my chamber. You aren't a servant." He set the dress on the back of the chair and then sat on his bed.

"It's something I do when I am... anxious," she replied.

"I thank you, but I want you to know it isn't necessary."

Jak slid out from behind the bed and walked to the dress. She pulled it from the chair and carried it to the door.

"No, change here while I sweep up the mess. I don't know that I will find shoes to fit you anytime soon."

Jak waited until he closed the door separating them and then she looked at the outer door. She crept to it and opened it gingerly. The sounds of many voices floated toward her from somewhere down the hall. Suddenly, a heavy set of footsteps stomped closer and she shut the door quickly.

"Are you all right?" Stefan called.

Jak rushed back to the bed, dropped her nightgown and pulled the soft tanned leather jerkin over her head.

"Yes. Thank you." The leather slid down almost to her feet and she had to roll up the sleeves to be able to see her hands. The dress was crude in fashion, but warm and comfortable. She wondered just how young the girl was that wore the dress if it still hung almost twice as wide as she was. She walked back to the doorway, rubbing her hands together and then opened the door to see him throwing the shards of the plate and pitcher out the window.

He turned to her. "Good. It fits."

She gave him a tight smile and rubbed her arms to garner warmth in them. "It will do. Thank you."

"Are you cold? Let me light a fire." He moved toward her, and she backed up. His imposing frame loomed like a tower over hers. The heat of his body rolled toward her as he brushed past her to the fireplace. He placed several enormous logs into it and then lit the tinder underneath. Jak joined him where he crouched down, blowing on the small flames urging them to grow.

A loud groan emanated from her stomach, and she clutched at it as Stefan grinned.

"You're hungry."

She nodded.

"Let me finish getting the fire going and then I'll take you to get something to eat."

Without thinking, she touched his shoulder where the blood had dried. She pulled the fabric away from the wound to see that the cuts were not too deep. He stopped and turned to her, his expression unreadable.

She jerked her hand away. "I apologize. I just want to make sure it doesn't look inflamed."

For several minutes they stared into the flames without speaking. Jak wished that she hadn't thrown the pitcher at him earlier, she would have liked to have had some water to clean herself with.

"Why are you so warm, yet it's so cold in here."

Stefan shrugged. "I'm used to it I suppose." He looked her up and down. "Then again, possibly you are so cold because you are so tiny."

"I'm not tiny. I'm tall for a human female. I'm five foot eight."

A smile cracked his lips making her heart jolt.

He turned back to the fire and blew on it for a few more minutes while she warmed herself. When the flames licked up the sides of the logs he stood and headed into her room and lit the second fire. Jak stared at the logs. She hated that they used wood for warmth, but she understood the necessity. Without it, they would all freeze. She prayed that they used trees already felled instead of living trees, but she hadn't the heart to ask.

"Are you ready?"

She turned to find Stefan already in the doorway. A sudden wave of apprehension drifted over her. She didn't know what lay beyond. Or who. Suddenly, wasn't sure she wanted to. She'd met three Jätte in the last day and two out of them were not what she would call friendly.

"I wouldn't mind if you simply brought something here. Not that I expect you to wait on me or anything, it's just..." She couldn't make herself voice the words. She couldn't afford for him to realize her fears. To know might mean he'd take advantage of it.

"How about you stay warm by the fire, and I'll get some food and drink? I need to check on my father, anyway."

"What happened to your father?"

"Stabbed by a thief."

"Someone in your kingdom?"

"No. Someone in yours."

Jak swallowed hard. "I... I'm sorry. But surely a wound from a blade from Fairelle wouldn't possibly be big enough to cause any real damage."

Stefan nodded as his eyes saddened. "You are correct, it shouldn't have, and yet, it has. We think it was no ordinary blade."

Jak sat on the floor beside the fire and watched him go again. Stabbed by a human for the sake of material possessions. How awful. No wonder they'd come down that giant stalk.

CHAPTER FOUR

Stefan walked to his father's room. Inside, Clive stared at the king. He glanced up when Stefan opened the door and his droopy eyes filled with sadness.

"No change."

Stefan nodded. His gaze drifted to the soaked bed sheet covering his father's ever thinning form. "His fever hasn't come down at all?"

Clive shook his head and his entire body wobbled like a saggy empty bag. He'd once been a mountain of a Jätte, but ever since the death of his son, he'd done little more than tend to the king and wither away.

Stefan lifted the sheet. The smell of putrid flesh wafted out, and Stefan replaced the sheet. The fact that his father had survived this long was a testament to his willpower. He only wished that there were more he could do.

"The men say Ivan brought back a healer from the ground."

"Not a healer, just a girl."

Clive's expression darkened. "Is there anything she can do? Women seem to know how to do a great many things that we do not."

Stefan couldn't disagree with the statement. "It's why they left. They knew we relied on them for everything. Just look at our crops and food stores."

"Not to mention the state of our clothing." Clive pointed to Stefan's ripped sleeve.

"How did we get like this?" Stefan mused. "When did we lose the ability to be self-reliant? I'd leave too if my spouse couldn't do anything for themselves."

"Especially protect them from invaders."

Stefan's gaze slid to Clive. "That was a setup from the beginning."

Clive nodded. "Even so, it proved your mother's point."

Stefan thought about Clive's words for several minutes before speaking again. "Do you think we should give up? Go to another kingdom and pledge ourselves as servants?"

"No," Clive recovered. "I didn't mean—"

"I'm not asking to trap you with your words. I am asking your honest opinion. If my father doesn't make it, do you think we should give our lands over to another?"

"I was born here, and I'll die here. Leaving isn't what I want. What I want is to learn. To take back what we once had. To rebuild and to become a proud kingdom once more."

Stefan nodded. For as passive as his father was, one

thing he'd always stuck to was the belief that some things were women's work and some were men's and the two shouldn't mix or change. He wondered if given a second chance his father would change.

"We'll start tomorrow," said Stefan. "We'll go into the field and see about planting a new crop."

"But the last time we tried to get the men to tend them they were so lazy everything died."

Stefan nodded. "True, but I have a feeling I know someone who might help with that."

"Who?"

"The girl from the low ground. Jak has a way with plants. And perhaps having her here will give the men hope for the future and give them some motivation again."

"Why would she help us after what Ivan did?"

"I don't know that she will, but I'll ask all the same. We need to do something. The men have spent the last years wasting away. If we want any chance of thriving moving forward we have to do something. I'm done with just surviving."

Stefan's father coughed and choked. Stefan rushed to lift him off his pillow as Clive grabbed a glass of water and held it to the king's lips. Julius sipped the water and breathed a bit easier. His eyes fluttered open for a moment before closing again.

"Father?" Stefan held his breath and waited, but the only reply was his father's labored breathing.

"I fear he's not much longer for this life."

Stefan's chest squeezed, and he lay his father back on his pillows. "Get Jethro to change the top sheet and pillowcases for my father. You change the bandages to something clean and rinse the wound again."

"Yes, Highness."

Stefan had seen battle wounds before, and from the sight and smell of his father's injury, they had less than a week before he would be gone if they didn't get a miracle.

Stefan balanced a tray of food on his left arm as he pulled the key from around his neck and put it in the lock of his door. The door next to his opened and Ivan stepped out. The two shared a tense moment before Ivan headed past.

"Where are you going?"

"Are you going to forbid me from eating as well?"

"Eat, and then get back to your chamber."

Ivan stopped and turned to Stefan. "You know you aren't my mother or my father, right?"

"And a good thing too because mother would've beaten you unconscious for taking Jak."

"Oh, Jak is it?"

"Yes, her name is Jak, and she happens to be a decent person despite what you did."

"And is *Jak* going to help father?"

"She can't."

"She can. She healed the garden plants, and I watched her uproot a tree and dump it on my head. She has magic."

"Not the kind we need for healing. You would have been better to grab the stupid human who did this to him. Instead, your hotheadedness did nothing more than take an innocent girl and force her to stay here against her will."

Ivan's gaze moved to the tray of food. "Doesn't seem too bad from where I stand. Seems she is getting the best pieces of meat and the last of the potatoes."

Stefan's grip tightened on the tray and he gritted his teeth. "After what you've done, I'd give her the whole damn pig if she asked."

Ivan's face broke into a lopsided grin. "You fancy her."

A need to lie ripped through Stefan's gut. "I simply feel responsible for her and her current situation."

Ivan snorted. "Of course. That must be it." He plucked a piece of ham from Stefan's plate and folded it into his mouth. "Give her my regards." He turned and headed down the hallway. "You're welcome."

"For what?" Stefan called.

Ivan turned around but continued to walk backward. "If it weren't for me, she wouldn't be snug in your chamber." Ivan stuck up his middle finger before jumping down the stairs.

Stefan clenched his jaw. If he hadn't been holding the tray he would have run after Ivan and thrown him back in his room like a spoiled tot.

His door opened a crack, and a set of bright eyes peered out at him. "Is everything all right? You unlocked the door several minutes ago."

Stefan gave her a tight smile. "Sorry. My brother and I were just having a… discussion."

She opened the door wider. "There are a few things I'd like to discuss with him myself."

"Unfortunately, he's gone." Stefan walked forward, and she backed up letting him in.

Jak closed the door behind him as he set the tray down on his bed. She regarded the bed, and before he could help her up, she grabbed the duvet, stuck her foot on the sideboard, and hefted herself up.

"You're like an apina." He chuckled.

"A what?" She took the oversized plate and set it in her lap.

"An apina. Don't you have those on the ground?"

She shrugged. "What do they look like?"

"They're small and furry with long fingers and tails. They climb trees and vines the way you do."

"I remind you of a small hairy creature with long fingers and a tail?"

"No, I didn't mean it like that. I simply meant the way you climb reminds me of them."

She cocked an eyebrow at him. "Uh-huh."

Embarrassment heated his cheeks.

Stefan picked at his plate for a moment trying to think of something to say as Jak devoured her food.

"Can I ask you something?"

"Yes." She licked her fingers.

"You seem... strangely resigned to being here. I mean, I'm glad you aren't throwing things at me anymore and that you didn't try to go out the window again, but you seem to be taking this whole, giants-in-the-sky thing rather well."

She shrugged. "Down in Fairelle I'm an outcast from my village for being half a dryad. I'd been visiting my Fae friend, Olivia, when your brother took me. I feel more kinship toward her than anyone else on the ground. I've heard tales of werewolves, vampires, merpeople, mages, daemons, and so many other races of creatures and people though I've never met any. I myself can talk to trees and plants. Not much surprises me now."

"And being here? I mean, if I were to be captured, I would do anything I could to escape, but you gave up with so little effort."

"You want me to go back out the window?"

"That's not what I mean."

She smiled, making the corners of her eyes crinkle. "You need to learn when people are teasing you." A tinkle of laughter escaped her lips. "To answer your question. I was on my way home when I was grabbed, but I didn't necessarily want to go there."

"Because of being an outcast?"

"Actually, the opposite. Because someone wanted me."

"And that's bad?"

"It is with that man," she sighed and picked at a piece of meat. "Whom I told half a dozen times I did not want to marry him, but he didn't care. Instead of finding someone else he made a wager with my father."

"A wager?"

"My father likes to drink and play cards, but he is terrible at both. So, he bet my hand in marriage in a game of cards. He won. I lost."

"Your father lost you in a card game like a prized steed?"

Her eyes widened at his disgust. "He said it was the cow or me. I like thinking I was a steed more than a simple cow. Rupert promised to pay off my father's debts and give him a monthly stipend to keep him happy and drunk. Meanwhile, I was to play dutiful wife and mother."

"From what little I know of you I'm sure you didn't take the news well."

"I think I took it quite well all things considered. I simply went into town and informed Rupert I wouldn't be honoring the deal and when he refused to listen, I tied him up and left him there."

Stefan broke out laughing. She laughed as well.

"You tied him up?"

"With vines and tree roots. I'm afraid I made quite a mess of the tavern in the process."

Stefan laughed even harder. "I would have loved to see that."

"So," she continued. "As you can see, I am not so keen on going home just yet."

Stefan's laughter died away. "Do you think he will hold you to that if you go back?"

"If I don't, my father is sure to kick me out and then where will I go?"

"Your father sounds like... an unkind man."

"That is a very gracious way of putting it. I take it your father is not unkind. I mean, your brute of a brother came down to the ground and snatched me in the night to help heal him."

"My father is a great man. Unfortunately, he has not been such a great king, I am realizing."

"How so?" She popped a piece of potato into her mouth.

"He relies too much on the traditions of the past. Refusing to move forward. It's those traditions that are killing our kingdom."

"Traditions are usually wonderful things passed on through a family, what is it you find so distasteful?"

"He believes a woman's purpose is to bear children and tend to the home. Because of that we men never learned how to do much more than raise crops and fighting. We didn't learn to mend clothes or cook, either. But since the women left, the men haven't been motivated to do much more than keep breathing."

"Then where did you get this food?"

"We bought it."

"Well, at least you have money to buy what you need."

"Not much I'm afraid. Between having to pay a premium on goods from other lands, and been invaded by the thief from the low ground..."

Stefan's gut clenched, and his gaze dropped to the bed. "I'm not quite sure how my father has hung on as long as he has. He's been hotter than the sun for a week now, and the wound looks worse each day."

"Have you been changing the bandages, flushing the wound, and applying fernblend to it?"

"Changing yes and bathing him every day or so. I don't know what fernblend is though."

"You must cleanse the wound, not simply bathe him. You must scrub it out if it is as bad as you say. Get all the bad tissue out until it bleeds red."

"What is fernblend?"

"A plant. It grows all over down in Fairelle. It's small and shaped like a fan with bright green leaves."

Stefan wracked his brain to remember if he'd ever seen

a plant like that. "There are some woods not far from here. Would you go with me?"

She nodded. "I could do that."

Stefan smiled. "It's late now. You should rest. Tomorrow we will head out."

Jak nodded and yawned.

"I've kept you up too long. You've had an exhausting day. I should let you rest."

Jak slid from the bed, her jerkin lifting and revealing her long slender legs. Stefan swallowed hard and turned away, ashamed for looking at her so. She remained under his protection, and that protection might just need to include himself.

CHAPTER FIVE

The following morning, Stefan awoke early and set about his business before Jak arose. First thing, he checked on his father who'd ceased being conscious at all. He then went down to the cells in the basement and gave Galin another thorough tongue-lashing for following Ivan to the ground and kidnapping Jak. He sentenced him to one more night in the cells and left him with a plate of food. Stefan hated to do it. Galin wasn't known for his wits, but he couldn't afford to allow his men to follow Ivan without fear of reprisal.

Lastly, he went to the kitchen and fixed Jak a plate of food and returned to her. He set it on the table in his room as she unlocked her chamber door and entered. The realization that she'd locked it in the first place sucker punched him in the gut. Did she think him capable of hurting her, or had it been reflex? He hadn't the heart to ask.

"Did you sleep well?" he asked.

"I've never slept in a bed so massive or so soft. I almost feared I would be swallowed whole."

He chuckled. "I used to feel the same as a small child."

She cocked her head to the side. "I'm having a hard time picturing you as a small child. A substantial sized child perhaps, but never small."

"Small is a relative term, I suppose. I can imagine you being quite a tiny thing yourself."

Jak sat at the table and peeled the boiled egg on her plate. "When should we head out for the herb?"

"We could go as soon as you finish eating."

Jak's gaze traveled to the door.

"I won't let anything happen to you."

"I'm not afraid." Her voice came out strong, but her eyes belied the truth.

"Even so, I want you to know that you have my word. As long as you are here in Luften, no harm will come to you."

She stared at him for a long moment and for a split second he thought he caught a glimmer of affection upon her beautiful face. Stefan's heart warmed at the thought that such a beautiful, fierce creature could possibly hold any caring for him.

He pushed the idea from his mind and broke the shell on his egg. He shouldn't think of her that way. They were from two different worlds. Hell, he was twice her size. If he tried to lay upon her, he might very well crush her as kiss her. And hurting her was the last thing he wanted to do.

"So, will we walk?"

Stefan lifted his gaze and smiled. "No. We shall take my steed. He's faster."

. . .

Stefan strode down the upper hallway with Jak, trying to keep her as tight to his side as he could manage without actually touching her. She was brave, he'd give her that, but even so, she wasn't strong enough to take on a Jätte, at least outside of a forest.

They descended the staircase to the floor below. The stairs opened into a spacious atrium that had lain barren for years.

Jak peered over the railing. "That's terrible."

Stefan followed her gaze to the inner garden that had once flourished, but now lay as a desolate reminder of all they'd lost.

"Indeed." Several of his countrymen stopped in the atrium and turned their eyes upward at them. Stefan coughed and continued to the next staircase.

"Do they all live in the castle?"

Stefan shook his head. "This is a keep. My brother, father and myself live here along with a few of the other men. Most live in the village. However, without much to do all day, everyone tends to gather here for meals as well as drinking and gambling."

"How sad that they have nothing better to do with their time." Her words carried an edge to them that he assumed was due to her father's own gambling and drinking.

"After their women left, a group of the men began taking out their anger on nearby kingdoms. But when their raiding parties were beat back, most of them felt utterly useless. They no longer had the respect of anyone. Not their enemies. Not their wives. No one. Soon, they just couldn't bring themselves to do more than the bare minimum and I couldn't blame them. But enough is enough. I'm tired of simply staring at the stars, riding Pasha and trying to keep everyone fed."

They continued down to the first floor and crossed the atrium. Jak stopped by the raised bed of dead plants and dug her fingers into the parched dirt.

"The soil is fertile if you would tend it. You could grow any number of things in this bed."

"What about the fernblend you mentioned?"

She nodded. "Possibly. It will spread rapidly so you'll need to keep it in check. But it is the most useful of all the herbs in Fairelle."

"Fairelle?"

"The world below. There are many different kingdoms, but the whole is called Fairelle."

"Fairelle." Stefan tried out the word. He'd only ever been taught it was called Low Ground.

The feel of several sets of eyes made Stefan lift his gaze. Half a dozen men stared at him and Jak.

"We should get going."

She nodded and stood, brushing off her hands. "If your men clear away the dead foliage and water the dirt, we could plant some fernblend when we return. Provided we find some."

Stefan smiled to himself. Already she helped them.

He called the men over to do as she'd instructed. The men regarded her with interest mixed with concern, but Jak looked as if it didn't bother her at all.

He and Jak continued to the entrance as the sounds of men pulling out the dead foliage shook the ground.

Stefan pushed open the front door, and Jak held up her hand to shield her eyes.

"It's so much brighter up here," she said. "I hadn't thought of that."

Stefan stared down the massive stone staircase.

"Would you like me to carry you? I don't want you to stumble."

Her gaze slid his direction. "I can manage, thank you."

He nodded. "Suit yourself."

Stefan began down the steps toward the village. The sun warmed him all over as he strode downward. Halfway down he stopped and glanced back for Jak. As there was no railing to hold onto, Jak made her way down the oversized steps gradually, trying not to stumble. Stefan suppressed a smile and waited. He couldn't push her. She was a girl used to doing things for herself. He respected that. His mother had been the same, though his mother had lacked the kind disposition that accompanied Jak.

When she caught up to him, he gave her a minute to catch her breath.

"You can see everything from up here."

Stefan nodded. "Our lands extend as far as you can see, but there isn't much outside the village down below. We used to have farms to the left, but they've not been tended to in over three years. To the right used to be grazing land but we've sold almost all of our cattle off to buy provisions."

Jak stood there and shook her head.

"What?"

She looked up at him. "For as big as you are it's as if you are children needing your mommies to tell you what to do."

Her words were a right hook to the jaw, but she wasn't wrong.

"Have you always been so... inept?"

"Luften was once the strongest kingdom in all the nations, but my grandfather believed tending to the home was woman's work. He spent most of his time raiding other kingdoms and taking over. That ended when he died, and the other kingdoms fell back to their rightful rulers under my father. But the tradition of women's work never did change. Hence the current predicament. Believe me I'm not blaming the women for leaving. It's all our fault for allowing things to deteriorate as far as they have."

"And there aren't any women willing to help you? Even for pay?"

Stefan started down the last leg of stairs. "They don't want to be associated with such a weak kingdom. They fear that doing so would open them up to being taken advantage of by others."

"I can understand that. Just because I keep to myself and I'm a peaceful person by nature, there have been those in the past who've thought they could take advantage of me."

Stefan held out his hand for her and helped her down as they approached the final step.

"Perhaps I could help you restart your crops," she offered. "Provided you own seed to grow and men willing to till the ground and take care of them of course. As I will not be here long enough to see a crop come in."

"Perhaps we could offer you some coin in exchange, so when you return to the low ground, you won't be beholden to your father or the contract he has set upon you."

Jak stopped walking for a moment, grabbed her waist as if searching for something and then blew out a breath. "Son of a—"

"What is wrong?"

She looked up at him and after a moment she smiled. "Nothing. I would be amenable to the offer of coin for my services. Thank you."

Stefan smiled to himself. He hadn't even had to ask her for her help. Instead, she offered it willingly. Her kindness knew no bounds. He wanted to ask her if she was really all right when the look of frustration refused to leave her face, but he didn't want to pry. If she wanted to tell him, she would.

They strolled through the village with every pair of eyes on them. It was strange, with Jak at his side it was as if he saw the kingdom for the first time. The houses were in disrepair. All the gardens seemed to be barely hanging on. Warthogs and chickens wandered around foraging in the rocks and dirt making him wonder how they were even still alive. For the first time in his life, he was ashamed of Luften. Of what it had once stood for and what it had become.

"I've never seen animals that large before. I suppose everything up here is bigger."

He shrugged. "I've never been to the low ground before, so I wouldn't know."

"Never?"

"Everything I want is here in Luften. Though it seems to be a bit more worn."

"You could use some improvements. If for nothing else, so the men aren't hurt. No one likes having their roof fall in on them while they're sleeping."

He snorted. "I'm sure they don't."

They made their way toward the stable with her pointing out places that could be improved. How the roofs could be made to grow flowers and grass on top to keep them cooler in the summers. How planting trees around would help with shade as well. She pointed out a sizeable dirt area that could be turned into a pen for the hogs and next to it a place for coops for the chickens so they could collect eggs easier. It seemed for every problem they faced Jak knew a way to help. Whatever they ended up being able to pay her, would never be enough.

JAK COULDN'T UNDERSTAND HOW THE JÄTTE COULD LET their kingdom fall so far. She hated being critical, but it was as if they were just waiting out their days until they died.

She followed Stefan into the stable, the only structure not in disrepair. The scent of hay and manure stung her nose.

As she passed the row of all-white animals, they stuck out their heads one by one. Jak stopped dead and stared. It couldn't be. It wasn't possible.

"What's wrong?" asked Stefan.

"Your... your horses have wings."

"Yes, they are pegusai."

One animal loomed over Jak, pushing its head forward almost knocking her over. Stefan chuckled and pet the pegusai's nose.

"She likes you."

Jak's heart hammered. "Are... you sure she doesn't just think I'm lunch?"

"Pegusai are herbivores like regular equines."

She stared at the beautiful animal who watched her intently. Jak took a step forward and held out her hand. The pegusai pushed its nose into her palm, and she smiled. Stefan stood next to her with an amused expression on his face.

"She's so soft." Jak ran her hand up the animal's nose to her ears and down her shoulder. "She's amazing. Where do they come from?"

"Pegusai are gentle animals. They were captured by a rival kingdom and made to work as slaves. My grandfather freed them and brought them here."

"You saved them." There was so much more to Stefan than she'd anticipated.

"We do our best to care for them and keep them safe, but it's difficult now. Feeding them costs a lot, and we can't let them go out to graze for fear of them being stolen."

"Why don't you plant grass inside the village? The area back by the stairs is wide enough for them to graze and then some. They'd be safe inside the walls, and it would give them a chance to get some exercise. I'm sure they don't like being cooped up in here all the time."

"We have no way to plant grass by the steps. We have a little seed, but it's not enough to cover the area."

She could do it. She could grow the seed for them. Why was she so eager to help? Why wasn't she kicking and screaming to be let go? Why wasn't she fighting to get home no matter what was waiting there for her? Why was she trying to help save the king? Peace fell over her as the pegusai looked deep into her eyes. The answer was simple, something about the place rung familiar. Like a long lost dream she couldn't quite catch long enough to remember. Yet it remained, and she knew somehow, she was connected to the place.

Jak's hand slid from the pegusai. "Where is your mount?"

Stefan pointed over his shoulder. "He's back this way."

They headed down the dozen stalls and stopped at the largest of the pegusai. Stefan dipped his head and pressed it against the animal's.

"Hello, Pasha."

The animal closed its eyes and stood for a moment. Then he reared back and pawed at the ground.

"I know. I'm sorry. I've been busy."

The animal shook his head making his snowy white mane shimmer.

"No, he isn't any better I'm afraid. That's why we need to ride out. Jak says there is a plant that might help heal him. It's in the Tungen Wood."

The animal turned his gaze upon Jak, and she swallowed hard.

"This is Jak. Short for Jakleen. She's from the low ground."

Pasha swung his head to Stefan again.

"Long story. Will you help me, old friend? Will you take us to the forest to search for the plant?"

Pasha nodded.

Stefan unlocked the stall and Pasha marched out, passing the other pegusai and touching each of them with his nose.

"You talk to animals?"

Stefan looked down at her. "You talk to plants?"

She snorted. "Point taken."

"The answer is no. I don't talk to animals. Pasha is king of the pegusai. He has the ability to talk to me."

"Fascinating."

"Let's hurry before he grows impatient and takes off without us." Stefan strode toward the exit.

"Wait. Takes off? You mean... flies?"

Stefan nodded. "It's the fastest way."

Jak swallowed hard and fought to keep on her feet as her vision blurred slightly.

"Are you all right?"

Jak forced a smile and nodded. "Mmhmmm."

Stefan walked back to her and looked over her. "You don't look so good."

"It's just that me and heights... we aren't really on the best of terms."

"But you climbed out the window."

"Because you kidnapped me. I didn't know what you would do after what I'd experienced with your brother."

"Technically I did not kidnap you, but that doesn't matter right now."

"No, it does not."

He placed his warm hand on her shoulder. "Remember? I won't let anything happen to you."

"You may be able to save me from a savage horde, but I doubt very highly you have a way to keep my heart from stopping in terror."

He gave her a gentle smile. "Come on." He held out his hand for her and Jak slid her hand into his despite the terror that raced through her.

They headed for the exit, meeting Pasha just as he finished saying hello to the last of the pegusai.

Pasha trotted into the sunshine and unfurled his wings to an immense expanse. He beat them several times, kicking up dirt and rocks. Several of the Jätte stopped to watch as Stefan led her toward the animal.

"I'm going to put you in the front. You are to sit forward as much as possible right behind the wing joint. Then I'll get up behind you."

Jak glanced at Pasha who stood majestically awaiting them. "What... what do I hold onto?"

"Grab his mane."

"Won't I hurt him?"

"Not that low on his neck. It's like the hair at the base of your skull. It takes a lot of force when you pull to actually hurt."

Jak nodded. She could do this. Wait why had she agreed to do this again?

Stefan moved close to her. "I'm going to lift you now."

His hands wrapped around her waist as he lifted her off the ground and set her on Pasha's back. She grabbed Pasha's hair and hung on as tight as she was able with her thighs.

"Scoot forward."

She scooted just behind Pasha's wings, her knees resting right where the wings met the hide.

Stefan reached around her and grabbed Pasha's wing joint and slung himself up behind her.

Pasha whinnied.

"I have not gained weight. If anything, I've lost weight," said Stefan. "Maybe you're getting old."

Pasha let out an indignant huff, and Jak laughed, easing her nerves somewhat.

"Let's get a move on."

Stefan slid closer to Jak, his entire body wrapping around hers like her own personal body armor. He grabbed Pasha's mane right below where she held on. The warmth and feel of his body so close to hers made her body tingle. His warm breath fell on her neck making her stomach clench.

Pasha beat his wings several times, and Jak fell back against Stefan's chest as Pasha's powerful legs pushed off the ground.

"Don't worry. I've got you," he said close to her ear.

The wings beat sharp and hard as they propelled the group into the air. For a split second, she thought she might throw up, followed immediately by the need to scream. The higher they got from the ground the more the urge to scream scratched up her throat and stuck to the roof of her mouth.

"Breathe."

Jak pressed her eyes shut tight. Her head began to pound from lack of air, and then Stefan slipped his bulky arm around her torso.

"You need to breathe, or you'll pass out. You don't want that to happen."

Jak sucked in air letting the cold wind rush into her lungs, waking her up.

Finally, they straightened out, and she listened to the rhythm of Pasha's wings beating.

"That's the old mill. And over there is Tinbar Lake where we used to fish. If you look straight ahead the woods are only a few minutes off. And beyond lay several other kingdoms."

Stefan continued to talk to her, but it was all lost on the fact that she couldn't bring herself to open her eyes.

Finally, as her heartbeat began to regain its normalcy, they dipped downward. Without thinking she grabbed onto Stefan's arm. He pulled her in closer to his chest, and she threaded her arm through his and nuzzled her head into the crook of his elbow.

"There's nothing to worry about. We'll be on the ground in a moment."

She nodded but couldn't speak. Terrified, she continued to squeeze her eyes shut until Pasha's feet touched the ground. All tension released and every muscle, which she hadn't realized had been tight as a lute string, relaxed a fraction. Relief washed over her like spring rain and even so, tears threatened to spill as her body shook like she'd just used too much magick.

Stefan slid from Pasha's back and looked up at her. "Are you going to be sick? You appear quite pale."

"I'll be fine once I feel the ground beneath my feet again."

He lifted her to the ground. She wobbled as dizziness threatened to topple her and he gripped her waist, steadying her.

"Easy. I have you." He pulled her into his body and pressed her cheek to his rock-hard abdomen. She clutched at him, sucking in air and willing her heart to cease pounding.

A horse. She'd been flying through the sky on a horse's back. The words alone made no sense, let alone the idea of it.

Eventually, she took a step away from Stefan and tried to focus on his face. She'd not noticed before how pronounced his chiseled cheekbones were. Where Ivan's brow had been heavyset, Stefan's was more refined. He sported plump lips, and a thin layer of stubble upon his chin.

Without thinking she reached up and ran her fingers through the ends of his wind-tousled hair hanging below his shoulders. Stefan stiffened but didn't move away. His hair slid through her fingers like silk. She pulled her hand away as the world came crashing down around her once more and reality set back in.

"I'm sorry. I didn't mean to do that. Your hair just looked so..."

"Seems only fair. I've had my arm around you for the

better part of twenty minutes. It's only right that I should allow you to touch me in return."

Jak swallowed hard at the intensity of his gaze. Men always looked at her. Some with fear. Some with loathing. Some with lust. But she'd not yet met one that gazed at her the way Stefan did. With a mixture of joy and something else she couldn't place.

Pasha whinnied, and Stefan stepped away and nodded. "Yes. Feel free to roam, but not too far. Hopefully, we won't be too long."

Pasha padded away through the trees.

Jak finally came to her senses. They had work to do. This wasn't some lazy afternoon walk in the woods with a lover. They were here for a purpose. To save Stefan's father.

Jak knelt to the ground and dug below the thick layer of moss and leaves to the dirt. She pushed her fingers into the rich wet soil and closed her eyes. For several moments she allowed herself to revel in the life pulsing around her. The imposing trees. The delicate, vibrant orange moss. The thick, ropey vines flush with blushing purple flowers.

"What are you doing?" asked Stefan.

"I'm feeling."

"Feeling what?"

She held out a hand to him. He looked at it and then took it in his own. She pulled him to his knees and pressed his palm to the ground. They sat quietly for several minutes.

"Can you feel it? It's so loud here. Like… like I can hear everything."

"Uh..."

"The life. Every creature, plant, animal, person, has a

life force. The trees are the strongest here, but if you listen, you can hear the others whispering. The moss shakes with worry of being trampled. The vines fear we will cut them from the trees and use them to make rope. The trees themselves are curious what we are doing here and wonder if we will take all their fruit and leave none for the animals. I've never felt it so strong and so... inviting. Like they want me to be here."

His gaze traveled over her face and an expression of wonder planted there.

"You really can hear them."

"Did you think I lied?"

"I... didn't know what to think. But I thought you said you couldn't communicate with them."

"No. I said it was different. Their language is much more primitive here. Now that I have a bit of feel for it, I know to simplify things. Watch."

Jak looked at one of the vines wrapped around a tall tree. She held out her hand to the vine, and it unwound from the tree and tapped Stefan on the shoulder. Stefan laughed. The vine slid up Stefan's neck and weaved itself through his hair.

"This is not at all strange," he laughed. "Like being pet by a tree."

Jak giggled at the uneasy expression on Stefan's face. A screech and mocking sound started high in the tree. It bounced around until the air rang with the piercing sounds. Jak peered high in the branches and spotted them. Small furry creatures with bright round eyes and long prehensile tails swinging from tree to tree.

"Apina," Stefan said.

Jak watched them for several minutes in awe of their abilities. They used their tails as if it were another hand. Swinging from branch to branch and vine to vine. They ran and chirped and screeched and finally calmed down and went silent once more.

"I hope I don't sound that bad."

Stefan winked at her. "Only when clinging to the side of a castle."

She waved at the vine, and it resumed its position on the tree. Following the vine, she set her hand upon it. Her magic flowed out of her finger, and in a burst, the vine grew twice as tall and twice as thick. Jak stumbled away.

"What happened?"

The vine grew taller and out of sight.

"My magic is stronger here. As if..." Jak stepped to the tree. It wasn't possible. It couldn't be. Her hand hovered inches from the tree, and without even touching it she could feel it pulsing with life.

"What is it?" Stefan asked.

Jak set her hand on the tree. The life force pulsed through her and her magic burned bright inside her like a thousand torches had lit in her veins. She touched the trunk again reaching out with her magic. Her mind whizzed through the forest cataloging everything at once. The trees, the plants, the animals, even—

Jak blinked as tears formed in her eyes. "This is my home wood."

Stefan shook his head. "I don't understand."

"This wood. My mother tree lives here."

CHAPTER SIX

Stefan stared at her for a long minute. "Your mother tree?"

Jak spun in a circle looking around wildly. "She's here. She has to be here."

"Your mother?"

Her eyes rounded. "It's why I've never found her. Never felt connected to the Low Ground or the people there. Because I am not from there. I'm from here."

Stefan shook his head. "I'm confused."

Jak moved to the nearest tree and placed her palm on it. "My mother is a tree dryad. Every dryad's spirit is connected to a tree. They return to the tree as their home."

"So, you have a home tree?"

"No, I'm only half dryad." Her mouth dropped open. "Maybe that's it. My mother had nowhere to keep me. I have no tree of my own in which to hide in if need be. But down there on the ground at least with my father, I would have shelter. Have you ever seen a dryad here?"

"No." He tried to understand her words. She was so excited he hated to dampen any of her spirit but... how could that be possible? "So... you're from Luften?"

Tears filled her eyes, and she nodded. "I must find her. Talk to her. Ask her all the things I've always wondered."

"But how?"

"The trees. They will show me the way."

A twig cracked. Stefan grabbed Jak's arm and pulled her close.

"What is it?"

"Shhhh." He peered into the trees and reached for his battle axe, but he hadn't brought it. "Damn." *Stupid, Stefan. Going out without a weapon.*

He scanned the dense forest, but no one emerged.

"Someone's here," she said. "The trees are quaking."

"We need to go. Now."

"But we have to find the fernblend."

Jak pressed her hand to the tree again and concentrated. She cocked her head to the side, and Stefan scanned the area once more.

"Found it." Jak ran north.

"Jak!" he whispered. "Jak stop!"

She continued to rush through the trees. Stefan looked over his shoulder. He needed to find Pasha. Torn, he struggled to decide which to do first. A whinny sounded far off, and Stefan ran in the direction of the noise. Again, there was a whinny and a screech.

Stefan whipped through the trees as branches tore at his

tunic and dug into his skin. He rushed into a small clearing of trees to find Pasha being set upon by two Jätte. They'd tied his two front legs with ropes and were pulling Pasha to the ground.

"Look at him," said the first.

"He'll make an amazing prize," replied the second.

Stefan barreled forward as the two continued to struggle with Pasha. He rushed the first man and knocked him to the ground, forcing him to let go of Pasha's rope.

"What the hell?"

Stefan smashed the Jätte in the nose. Blood gushed down the man's face, and he howled in pain as Stefan jumped to his feet and headed for the second man. But the second man spotted Stefan and let go of his rope just in time to spin away, making Stefan miss him.

"Go!" Stefan yelled. "Go back to the stable!"

Pasha took to the air, ropes dangling from his feet he flew out of sight.

"That wasn't very smart," said the second Jätte.

The first man got to his feet, blood staining his face and shirt. He pulled an axe from his belt.

"You're gonna pay for that."

Stefan stood his ground. "Possibly, but this is not a fight I think you want to start. I am Stefan, Prince of Luften."

The two men looked at each other and laughed. "You think that means anything to me? I'm Marius, heir to the throne of Kinline. Luften is nothing more than a dead village of dung sacks who can't even keep their women happy."

"I even heard that the king has given up and is finally dying."

"Enough." Stefan's fists clenched tight.

"Want to make me stop, your highness? Come on then. I haven't given out a good ass whooping in over a week now."

Stefan's gaze bounced between them. Taking them would've been easy a couple years prior. He'd studied fighting and wrestling since boyhood. But like everything else in the kingdom, those lessons had been sporadic at best in the past year. He was sure he could take one of them, but both might prove to be a bit challenging.

"Stefan?" Jak's voice floated from across the clearing and through the trees, making his stomach drop.

"Jak! Run!"

"A female?"

"I thought there weren't any left in Luften."

Marius glared at Stefan. "Go get her, Prentis."

Stefan charged Marius as Prentis took off. He tackled Marius to the ground before he could swing his hammer. Stefan punched the thieving Marius in the face, but Marius grabbed Stefan by the skull and head-butted him. Stunned, Stefan fell backward. He rolled over and struggled to get to his feet as pain spiderwebbed through his skull.

Marius spat blood on the ground and reached for his war hammer. Before he could grab it, Stefan kicked him in the rear sending him sprawling. Stefan snatched up the war hammer as Jak screamed. He turned to see her being dragged through the trees by her hair. Vines flailed and reached for her, unable to help in the confusion.

Marius rushed him, but Stefan swung the war hammer

handle at the man connecting with the side of Marius' head. Marius crumpled like a piece of dirty laundry.

Stefan hurled the war hammer at Prentis hitting him square in the chest, just as a large branch hurled through the trees and slammed into Prentis' head. He fell on his rear and Jak scrambled out of his grip.

"You big... big... dung beetle!" She kicked with surprising force, and connected with Prentis' nose. Blood splashed out of his nose as he toppled backward. Stefan rushed to Jak and picked her up.

"Are you hurt?" he asked, his heartbeat thundering.

"No." She clung to him tightly as the sound of beating wings descended from above.

Pasha landed unsteadily on the ground next to them, stumbling due to the ropes and Stefan ran to the steed. He set Jak on Pasha's back and then ripped the rope apart and threw his leg up.

"No!" Jak yelled. "The fernblend." She pointed back toward the downed Prentis.

Stefan slid from Pasha and ran to the where she pointed. Prentis sprawled on the ground trying to suck in breath. Next to him lay a bundle of plants. Stefan grabbed the greenery and hurried back to Pasha. He handed them to Jak and pulled himself up. Grabbing Pasha's mane, the steed took to the air almost sending Stefan flying backward.

Stefan glanced down as they lifted higher into the air. Marius struggled to his feet and Stefan wrapped his arm around Jak instinctively. She pressed her body into his and clutched his arm.

"They didn't hurt you, did they?" Stefan asked.

"Not but my pride," Pasha replied.

Stefan's heart still raced but relief washed through him the further they got from the ground. Safe. He needed to make sure Pasha and Jak were safe.

PASHA LANDED HARD, JOLTING STEFAN AND JAK AND MAKING Stefan grimace. As the adrenaline wore off, the pain began to settle into Stefan's face, chest and arms. Jak slid from Pasha's back and dropped to the ground. Her stomach lurched but stopped herself from throwing up.

Stefan dismounted, and his legs wobbled as he hit the dirt. He walked to Pasha's head and looked him over to make sure he wasn't injured.

"I'm sorry for putting you through that."

"It was worth it if it will help your father," replied Pasha.

Jak stood, and Pasha stamped his front feet.

"He's glad you are all right," Stefan said.

Pasha trotted toward the stable as Stefan helped Jak to her feet. Aside from being dirty she appeared otherwise unharmed.

"Why did they do that?" she asked.

Stefan shook his head. "Honestly, I don't know. I assume they stumbled upon Pasha and thought he would be a great prize, but the fact that they were so close to Luften concerns me more."

She reached up on her toes and touched his cheek. A twinge of pain mixed with a swirl of desire shot through him.

"You need that sewn up."

Stefan shook his head. "I'll be fine." He held up the plants. "We need to get these to my father. And I need to speak to my brother."

She nodded. "Let's hurry."

"WHAT IS SHE DOING?" IVAN DEMANDED.

"Shut up and let her work," Stefan replied.

Jak ignored them and continued to chew the bitter leaves as she bathed the festering wound in hot water. She knew better than to tell them how severe the injury was. Anyone in the room could smell the infection. Beyond that, the king's breathing was so shallow that more than once she thought he'd stopped breathing altogether. His skin held a waxy pallor as close to a death shroud as she'd ever seen. But worse than all that was the fact that he hadn't even made a peep since she'd begun to clean the wound.

Jak finished washing his wound and sat for a moment looking at it. The water and rag had turned a sickly yellowish green color, but the wound still oozed.

She spat the chewed leaves into a clean bowl and turned to Stefan.

"We need to scrub it."

He stared at her from behind his thick dark lashes, his eyes troubled.

"Do you know the kind of pain that will cause?" Ivan barked.

She gritted her teeth and ignored him as she awaited

Stefan's response. He looked at the other man, Clive. "Do it."

Ivan lunged forward. "No."

Stefan caught him by the arm and yanked him back.

"You said she wasn't even a healer. How do you know she isn't trying to kill him?"

"Because I believe despite everything, she wants to help. No thanks to you."

Ivan yanked his arm away. "Do what you think is best, but I tell you now if he dies-"

Stefan stood nose to nose with his brother. "What will you do?"

Ivan's eyes flickered to her and then back to Stefan. "You know I don't wish our father dead. I love him as I could love any father. But know that if he dies, in the state our kingdom is in now, we could lose half the men to dissent. Many have just been waiting for a reason to leave."

"So, what do you expect me to do?" asked Stefan.

"Give them a reason to stay." Ivan turned and walked out of the room.

Stefan stared at the spot for a moment before turning to her.

"What do you need me to do?"

CHAPTER SEVEN

Jak and Stefan exited the King's chamber and walked down the hall to their room. He unlocked the door and held it for her as she drooped with fatigue. With everything she'd been through in the past few days, everything she'd done, she wanted to drop into bed and sleep for a week.

"My men brought up buckets of water for the bath," Stefan said. "I figured you'd want to bathe before retiring."

"Thank you." She walked into the room and stopped by the already lit fireplace. She let the heat seep into her skin. The scent of dirt and blood permeated her clothing. She couldn't wait to get them off.

"I'll go see if I can find you something else to wear."

She turned as he headed out the door. "That's not necessary."

"I'm sure you don't want to sleep in that and your night dress is equally as dirty."

She could see how fatigue and sadness weighed on him as much as it did on her.

"I can wash my nightdress and hang it by the fire to dry before bed. You should bathe first. Then we can cleanse your wounds."

He shook his head. "You bathe. I'll find you something to wear. After we can tend to my wounds."

"Stefan—"

"Please!" He blew out a breath and gave her a tight smile. "Please. You are my guest. I would feel much better if you would bathe first."

She nodded at his sudden outburst. "If it would please you."

"It would." He stepped out the door and closed it.

The distinctive lock slid into place a second later. Her heart went out to him. She'd never experienced anything like what he was going through with his father, and yet she felt the soul-crushing weight anyway. She wanted to do him a kindness by letting him wash first, but she could see that his pride wouldn't allow it. Stefan wasn't prideful, yet he did derive satisfaction from being able to help and do for others. He had little, and yet, he gave what he had.

Jak entered her room and the bathing chamber beyond. She undid the tie on the leather jerkin and dropped it to the floor. She stared at the bath for a minute before stepping into the hot water and sinking into it.

A KNOCK ON THE BATHING ROOM DOOR PULLED JAK AWAKE.

"May I come in?"

Jak sat up suddenly and searched for something to cover herself with. How long had she been asleep? The water remained warm, though not quite hot. She spotted a fluffy yet faded piece of drying cloth hanging in the corner. She ran to it, wrapping it around herself just as the door opened.

"Jak? Are you alright?" Stefan spotted her and averted his eyes. "I apologize. I feared something may have happened to you. I found you some things to wear. I'll leave them out here by your bed if you'd like to dress."

"Come in." She pushed her long, wet hair over her shoulder.

"I don't think—"

"Sit on the edge of the tub so I can examine your wounds." It wasn't a request.

Stefan hesitated and then stepped through the door. He walked to the tub and sat on the edge. Jak met him eye-to-eye for the first time.

She took in his entire handsome face before dipping the bottom edge of her cloth into the water and touched it to his cheek. She wiped away the blood and dirt as he stared at the floor. Her stomach quaked at the nearness of his body. Every muscle in her fingers twitched to touch his skin.

"You are worried about your father."

He nodded.

She dipped the towel in the water again before touching it to his cut. His eye twitched, but he didn't make a sound.

"You've done everything you are able for him," she said. "You cannot worry about what you cannot change. It's in the hands of the gods now."

He nodded but still did not speak.

She cleaned his cut. "I could put some fernblend on this to speed the healing, but it's stopped weeping. Stitching it would be no use now."

"It'll scar, making me more fierce-looking."

"I suppose." She looked down at his arm where the sleeves of his tunic had been ripped open. "Take off your shirt."

His eyebrows knit together. "Excuse me?"

"Your shirt, take it off so I can clean the cuts on your arms."

"You don't need to."

"You saved my life. Twice. The least I can do to repay you is clean your wounds and make sure you do not end up in bed like your father. I don't think leaving your kingdom in the hands of your brother is the safest of ideas."

"You think my father is going to die." It wasn't a question.

"That's not what I said. But even you must know that that is a genuine possibility. His wound... I've not seen much worse."

Stefan lifted his tunic over his head and dropped it to the floor.

For several seconds all Jak could do was stare. Muscles upon muscles stacked beneath a dusting of dark soft moss looking curls. She wanted nothing more than to twirl her fingers through them. Instead she cleared her head, swearing at herself several times for being so stupid, and then inspected his torso. She pressed her palm into his side where a deep purple bruise sat. He winced, and she gently prodded the area until he grabbed her wrist.

Their eyes connected as warmth flooded through her.

"I think you may have broken some ribs."

"Only two or three. They'll heal."

He continued to hold her wrist in his grasp. Not hard, but with enough pressure to make her body flush with anticipation.

He searched her face. "You are so tiny." His voice came out husky and low. "Like if I applied even the slightest bit of pressure, I would break you in two."

A slight smile twitched the corner of her mouth. "I'm much heartier than I appear."

"You'd have to be to have survived both my brother and another Jätte attacking you."

For the next half hour Jak meticulously cleaned Stefan's wounds. Even when she felt they were sufficiently cleansed she couldn't bring herself to stop. Being near him left her with a sensation she had never experienced with another person. A feeling of belonging, of familiarity, of completeness. They didn't speak anymore, but the silence between them was not one of the jittery, uncomfortable kind people tried to fill with meaningless chatter. Instead, it was like a cocoon of peace between two beings who'd known each other their whole lives. Something that both appealed to her and terrified her at the same time.

After she could no longer prolong their time together, Jak left him to bathe. She walked into her chamber to find an entire oversized trunk full of clothing sitting at the foot of the bed. She dug around inside and removed dress after dress. It made no sense. They were all her size if not a bit short but definitely made for a human female. At the bottom, she found two dressing gowns made of silk. Far more luxurious and beautiful than anything she had ever owned. She pulled out a light peach one and rubbed the fabric between her fingers. It rolled like water on her skin. Without waiting another moment, she dropped her cloth to the ground and pulled the gown over her head. It slid down to her ankles and made her smile. The fabric caressed her bare skin, softer than her cow's nose back home.

Again, she dug through the trunk and found a hairbrush as well as several ribbons. She pulled the brush from the chest and tried to undo her tangles. A stubborn knot eluded her at the base of her skull, and she spent the better part of half an hour working to untangle it.

Her arms ached, making her stretch. The door to the bathing room opened, and Stefan stepped out in nothing but a drying cloth. His large muscular body sending a shiver over her skin. She stared at him for several seconds before clearing her throat and turning away.

"Can you possibly help me?" she asked.

"Anything."

"I... I have a tangle at the back of my hair that I can't reach."

He sat on the bed next to her and took the brush from her hand. His warm breath hit her neck making her skin pebble. His hand ran across her back as he lifted the hair and began brushing from the bottom. Little at a time he worked the brush higher and higher, section by section. The feel of his hands on her skin had her body pulsing with desire. She'd not experienced anything so sensual before.

Finally, he combed through her hair from scalp to end and rested his hand on her waist.

"Is that good?"

She ran her fingers through her hair with ease. "Thank you. I was afraid I might have to cut it out."

"That would be a shame."

Jak looked over her shoulder. His face loomed close to hers. She turned to face him more fully and slid her hand over to his. He leaned in and rested his face next to hers. He inhaled deeply and touched her hair again.

"You're like a Lila flower. So delicate and soft."

Tears threatened to spill as his words pierced her through the heart. "No one has ever said anything like that to me before." Her voice came out little more than a whisper.

"Do you think I jest?"

She shook her head and tried to form words. "No. I don't, but..."

"But what?"

Words failed her as too many thoughts coursed through her mind. "I'm unsure of how to respond. I never thought I'd hear such kindness directed at me."

His large bright eyes stared deep into hers. "You should be showered in kind words. Bathed in jewels and treasures. Worshiped day and night."

He loomed so close she could taste his breath on her tongue. His lips brushed hers ever so lightly sending a wild-fire through her. She wanted to feel his lips against hers. To feel the heat of his skin on her skin. The weight of his body pressing her into the sheets as his large calloused hands caressed her flesh.

Jak yanked away. What if she was too small? What if he broke her or crushed her?

Stefan rose quickly and turned away. "I apologize. I... I shouldn't have said those things."

"No. No, they were beautiful."

"I should go." He headed for the door.

"Stefan—"

"Please forgive me, Jak. I didn't mean to... I mean I shouldn't..." He blew out a breath. "Good night."

"Stefan!"

He stopped but didn't look back.

She fought for words to explain to him her fears... but the words wouldn't come.

"Thank you," she finally said. "For helping me with my hair."

"You're welcome."

Without another word, he left.

Jak slumped to her bed and tears flowed from her eyes. His gentle husky voice played in her head once more.

"You should be showered in kind words. Bathed in jewels and treasures. Worshiped day and night."

No man had ever wanted her as more than just a possession. And those that had, hadn't been a tenth of the man that her gentle giant was.

She remembered the terror when she'd been grabbed by the hair and dragged from the patch of fernblend that she'd been concentrating on. Calling out to the trees and having them reach for her, trying to help, but she'd been dragged too quickly into the clearing. She'd managed to find a large branch and hurl it at his head. Then the feel of Stefan's strong arms. The way he'd put her on Pasha first and shielded her in the air. How he'd whisked her straight up to their room and provided for her.

She stopped. *Their* room. Why did she consider it their room? She'd never actually had a room before, but she did have the cabin she was raised in. She supposed that was home. And... she did plan on going home, didn't she?

CHAPTER EIGHT

Jak awoke the next morning to the men moving around both inside and out of the castle. Hammering, yelling and sounds of people hard at work drew her to her feet. She snuck to Stefan's room, but he'd already gone. Heading back to her room she slipped into one of the dresses and went to the exterior door. She tried the handle and found the door unlocked for once.

She opened it a crack and peeked out, but the hall was empty. Again, voices floated from below, and she headed down the hallway toward them. As she hit the landing on the floor below, she witnessed men carting in fresh dirt into the empty atrium. Others spread it out and patted it down. All around, the Jätte washed floors and windows. Ivan barked orders making Jak's entire body clench in irritation. For several minutes she watched the commotion before Stefan's deep voice floated through the front door. He entered, followed by a tall, thin man carrying a basket full of small sacks. Stefan pointed to the atrium, and the man nodded. She watched Stefan march around complimenting the men on their work and correcting where necessary. So unlike Ivan, she could see the respect his men gave him.

As if hearing her thoughts, Ivan turned toward her.

"Her royal highness has decided she's had enough beauty rest," Ivan announced.

All eyes traveled to where she stood. A flush blossomed over Jak's body at the prying eyes, but she refused to be bullied by him any further.

"Is that what you call it? Then I suggest you go back to bed because you surely need it more than I," she retorted.

Several snickers and laughs abounded. Ivan's gaze narrowed on her but she didn't flinch.

"Careful lass or I'll be forced to teach you a lesson in manners."

"Don't forget if it weren't for me, you'd be dead under a tree right now."

"True, but I don't see a plant in sight for you to use your magic on."

"Do you not?" Jak looked down at the man sitting at the edge of the atrium separating sacks of seeds. She reached out with her magic and identified the dormant life inside the seed coats. She pushed her magic at a bag of seeds, forcing them to spring forth and grow. The Jätte stumbled away as the plants grew and twisted their way toward Ivan.

He stood his ground prepared for a fight as the plants snaked across the floor closing in on him.

"Jak, Enough," said Stefan.

Her gaze connected with his and what she saw there wasn't kindness, but it wasn't quite anger either.

"This is our problem," Stefan continued. "We would rather squabble amongst ourselves then do something about our predicament. Look at what this place has become. A rundown shell of its former glory. It's no wonder my father lays dying. What do we have to live for anymore? Or are we living at all? Maybe we are simply waiting around to die. No more. If you are waiting to die why wait any longer? Go to one of the other kingdoms and let them shoot you at the gate. Spread the word. Anyone who wants to stay in Luften will no longer be allowed to lazy about and hope something changes. Everyone will be expected to pitch in with the work. There is no more woman's work and man's work there is only work, and it will need to be done by everyone if we intend on surviving. Those who would rather complain or bicker are welcome to do so elsewhere."

A murmur spread across the hall like a wave crashing on the shore. Everyone waited for someone to say something.

Ivan scanned the room. "Well? You heard my brother. Work or get out."

One by one the men went back to what they'd been doing. The Jätte who'd been separating the seeds stared at the vines that had sprouted flowers as if they were contagious.

"Get them in the ground," Jak said. "And make sure their roots sink deep and water them thoroughly."

The man looked from her to Stefan. Stefan nodded and headed for the stairs. She caught Ivan's eye once more, but this time they weren't full of malice. This time he regarded her with a strange interest.

Stefan rounded the staircase, and she stepped back from the railing. He stared at her for a moment before speaking.

"Are you hungry?"

"I could eat."

He nodded. "There is food in the kitchen. Feel free to take what you like. As you can see, I have much to attend to today, so I won't be able to babysit you."

"Babysit me?"

"I'm sorry you're trapped here for the upcoming week and a half, but this time is critical to get the seeds planted and the men to work. Winter will be upon us before we know it and if we don't do this now, I fear many won't see next spring."

"Is there anything I can do to help?"

He shook his head. "Might be for the best if you occupy yourself in my rooms until the end of your stay. There is a library downstairs if you like to read. You may go out and find some books if you'd like."

"Your Highness?" A Jätte ascended the stairs toward them.

"I need to go." He turned to leave.

"Stefan?"

He ushered the other man on.

"Why are you being so cold?"

"I do not mean to be cold, Jak. I simply have a lot to do and very little time in which to accomplish it."

"Then let me help. You saw how I can make things grow."

He nodded. "Yes, impressive. But if my men are going to survive, they need to learn to depend on themselves and each other, not on magic and women. It was relying on women that got us into this in the first place."

Stefan trotted down the stairs and out of sight, leaving Jak feeling more alone than she ever had before. She'd thought she'd found a place of peace and rest, but from Stefan's words it sounded as if she were mistaken. When the stalk returned, she would be going back to Fairelle, the other world that no longer wanted her either.

STEFAN SPENT THE NEXT TWO DAYS GETTING THE CASTLE cleaned and the atrium planted with seeds. The section Jak had suggested be planted with grass seeds for Pasha and his herd had been tilled, and pens had been started for the live-stock. Getting all the men working again made him smile.

By afternoon he'd sent them off to work on their own huts. He wanted their roofs repaired and the outsides first. Weeds pulled, stones replaced, cracks patched, and windows cleaned. The dilapidated condition of the village just added to the dilapidated spirits of the entire kingdom.

The men complained about being sore, but for the first time, they did it with smiles on their faces. And for as many complaints as there were, they were outweighed two-fold by the compliments the men gave each other on how their repairs and renovations were looking. For the first time in a long time he sensed an air of hope amongst his kingdom.

Stefan climbed the stairs to his room with an increasing anxiety building in the pit of his stomach. He'd managed to avoid Jak by staying out late and leaving early, but as supper drew down upon them on the third day, exhaustion settled in his muscles like the rest, and there was nothing for it. He'd embarrassed himself days before with his flowery words. He hadn't meant to say and do all the silly things he had. It was ridiculous to think a sweet creature like Jak could see him as anything more than one of the kind who'd kidnapped her.

He stood outside his room with his hand on the door-knob unable to bring himself to open it. He'd not seen Jak in almost three days... he wasn't sure it had been enough time. The slap of the expression on her face after he'd declared his feelings still stung his skin. After a minute, he turned and headed to his father's chamber.

CLIVE SAT EVER FAITHFUL AT HIS FATHER'S SIDE.

"Any change?"

The man shook his head. "Not any good ones. The fever is higher and the wound worse again. I fear we were too late."

Stefan drew near his father's side and lifted the bed sheet. The wound seeped around the fernblend and deep veins spread across his torso.

"I'll stay with him again through the night," said Clive.

"I cannot thank you enough. I'll have someone bring up something for you to eat." His gut clenched as he beheld his father's face. "I fear it won't be long now."

Clive hung his head and settled back into his seat as Stefan turned and headed out. His heart sank with the realization. He'd so hoped the plant would work a miracle, but the truth stared him in the face. There were no miracles for them now.

He'd just closed the door when Ivan appeared.

"Is he better?"

"No."

Ivan nodded. "Then we must prepare for the end I fear."

Stefan noticed the plate Ivan held. "For Clive?"

Ivan breathed deep and held it out. "Actually, for you."

Stefan snorted. "Is it rotten?"

"Very funny. Can't I do something nice every once in a while?"

"I think every decade is your limit and you were nice to me last year if I remember. I lay sick, and you started my fire for me."

Ivan opened his mouth, shut it, and then opened it again. "I simply wanted to tell you I was... proud of you for what you've gotten the men to do in the past few days. I didn't think you had it in you."

"Had what in me?"

"The ability to lead. To not be like father. To think beyond your ideals and look at what is best for everyone. But you've proved you do have it in you to be a true Jätte leader. I was wrong for doubting you."

Ivan hadn't spoken to Stefan in such a kind way since before their mother left.

"I've never given you reason to believe in me before, I suppose," he finally said.

"But you can now. I believe in you, and the men respect you. You can turn Luften around. Make us proud again."

Stefan snorted. "I'd settle for self-sufficient."

"Either way. We won't have to always have our hand out for scraps from other tribes. Always laughed at. Mocked."

"That's my plan. Unless Father recovers, then it will be up to him."

"Will it?"

Stefan stared at his brother.

"You and I are both aware that all that's happened has been because of Father. Now is our chance, though. Our chance to change things. To show him there is another way."

"I won't betray our father, Ivan."

"I'm not speaking of betrayal; I'm talking about survival. You said yourself we won't make it another winter if we don't do this. Possibly this time with him incapacitated is what Luften needs to get back on its feet." He paused for a moment before continuing. "Mayhaps she is exactly what Luften needs."

"She?"

"Yeah. Your little tree fairy girl."

"She's a dryad."

"She's the reason you're trying to spruce this place up. So, she'll stay right?"

Stefan refused to admit it. "She may be the catalyst, but she isn't the reason."

"Well, whatever the reason, I'm glad for it. Last week I considered leaving Luften. But today..."

Stefan placed his hands on his younger brother's shoulders. "It would kill father if you left."

"Maybe, if he survives," said Ivan. "But staying here with how things are has been killing me. I don't want to be like this. I want a wife. Children. I want to build something I can be proud of. I don't care if it's furniture, weapons or an empire. If the only way to have those things is to move away and start over in a new kingdom with a new name, then that's what I'll do. And don't tell me you don't want the same things. If you didn't, I'm sure you wouldn't be getting as attached to Jak as you are."

Ivan handed the plate to Stefan and then went into their father's room before Stefan could reply.

Stefan hated to admit it but he did feel the same. After all this time. They'd never once spoken of what they wanted out of life and yet for as different as he and his brother were, they wanted the same thing.

Stefan mulled over his brother's words. What if their father woke up and he wanted it all to go back to how it was? As remote as the possibility seemed it was still there. Ivan was right. They needed to show their father, the men, and all of the kingdoms it could be different. They'd wallowed enough in their own pity. It was time to stand up and live again. Otherwise, they might as well be slaves. And to do that he must to do the one thing he didn't want to. Humble himself and ask Jak for help.

STEFAN SWALLOWED HARD AND ENTERED THE ROOM. Standing in the doorway he listened for a sound, but none emanated. Guilt seeped into his gut for neglecting her. It wasn't her fault she did not see him the same way he saw her. She was beautiful and gentle and he was nothing more than a big dumb oaf who couldn't even keep his men in line or grow crops without help. How pathetic she must think him compared to the men on the low ground. And now he was about to appear even more pathetic by asking her for help. He swallowed down his shame and guilt and squared his shoulders. It didn't matter. His pride couldn't matter. He had to think of his men and his kingdom. Pride had gotten them into this mess so it seemed only fitting that him humbling himself would get them out of it.

"Jak?" he called softly.

No answer.

"Jak?" he called again.

Inside her room, she was nowhere to be seen. For a split second his gaze traveled to the window in fear. She wouldn't have gone out there again, would she? The beanstalk wasn't due for a little over a week. She couldn't have left. Where would she go? He checked the window, but it was still locked.

Turning, Stefan set down the plate and strode out to the hallway, then down to the balcony. He looked into the atrium. Several of his men tended to the seedlings, watering them, digging about them, plucking any remaining weeds, but she wasn't there either. Stefan headed down the stairs.

After looking in the library, he searched floor by floor for close to twenty minutes without success. Anxiety had just begun to settle inside him when he made his way into the kitchen and found her sitting at a table reading a book and sipping from a bowl. Stefan thought his heart might stop at the sight of her so unaffected by his unease. She turned the page of her book and looked up, her face blank.

They stared at each other for a moment and then she sipped her soup again and went back to her book. Her hair was intricately braided and hung down her back. She wore a beautiful peach dress. He opened his mouth and closed it again, unable to form words.

"I made soup if you want some." She didn't look up.

The words didn't come out angry, only indifferent. He wasn't sure which was worse. Her being upset he probably could've handled because at least it would have shown she had some feeling toward him.

"What kind?" he finally asked.

She glanced up once more, one eyebrow cocked. "Does it matter?"

"Uh... no."

She went back to her book.

Stefan walked to the battered soup pot and spooned out a bowlful before taking a seat at the table. He ate silently for several minutes.

"What did you do today?"

She flipped the page. "Are we speaking now?"

"I... I didn't know we weren't."

She lifted her gaze. "I haven't seen you in almost three days."

"I've been busy." It was true he'd been busy, but more the truth that he'd kept himself occupied.

She turned the page. "Then what does it matter what I did? I stayed out of your way."

Stefan dropped his spoon in his bowl. "I'm sorry about saying those things. They were unjustified."

"They were."

"I... apologize."

She studied him for a moment. "Took you long enough."

Stefan smiled to himself.

She closed her book. "You and your men seemed to get a lot done."

"It's a decent start, but there's a lot needing to be done and not much time to finish."

"Because of winter?"

"No. Because if my father wakes up…"

Her brows furrowed. "I thought you wanted him to wake up."

"I did. I mean, I do. Ivan and I were talking—"

"You're taking Ivan's advice?"

"This time, yes, because he makes some sense. If we want things to change we need to show my father we can change, and want to change, by everything we've started."

She nodded. "Makes sense."

"But..."

"But?"

"It would work better if we were further along."

She set down her spoon. "Are you asking for help?"

"I have no right to, but I am."

She stared at the table for a long minute and a million comments raced through his head.

Finally, she looked up at him again, her eyes determined. "What do you need?"

CHAPTER NINE

J ak stood outside the outer gate, the rapidly darkening sky obscuring her view.

"You have been busier than I realized."

In the past days, Stefan had managed to get his men to clear an entire field for crops. Made pens for the animals. Begun to work on the huts. Started repairing the wall. And probably dozens of other things she couldn't see.

"I want to make a point, that the men could do this if they would just try. So, I needed to think big."

"I would say you are well on your way there." She scanned the field and breathed a sigh. "How big do you want them?"

"As much as you're able without hurting yourself."

Jak chuckled. "Unlike many magick users, I do not weaken from using my magick. The very magick I use to feed the plants and make them flourish grows in and of itself the more I am surrounded by plants and plant life. It's an endless well as far as I can tell."

"Have you ever tried to use it up?"

"Once. I wanted to be like normal people so badly that I tried to use everything I had. I grew a banyan tree from a seedling to what should've taken two hundred years to grow. By the time I'd finished, it'd grown as big as half my town. Took me sixteen hours and when I finished, I only slept for a day and ate three meals at once. But I was no more fatigued than if I'd simply walked the whole time."

"Why do you think that is?"

"No idea. If I'd been brought up by my mother, mayhaps I would know."

Jak took in her surroundings again. She strolled to the field, the sky now completely black.

"What did you plant?"

He snorted. "Honestly? I haven't a clue. We didn't know what the seeds were."

"Then how are you sure you planted them right?"

"What do you mean?"

"Corn needs to be planted in several rows, so they pollinate well. Vegetables like squash will spread out and strangle other plants. Pepper and tomatoes need to be propped up as do beans. And those are just a few."

"Well, I guess it will be a surprise to all of us then."

She moved to the first row of dirt and knelt on the ground. She pressed her fingers into the soil and allowed the cool moisture to invade her. Peaceful, calming vibrations snaked up her arms making her smile.

She reached out for all the life which permeated the

ground. Each signature registered within her. Surprisingly, the Jätte hadn't done too bad in their planting. The spacing was even and the crops sustainable. She prodded each seed with her magic, pushing them to grow. Their energy pushed back against her hands strengthening her and beginning the circle.

Jak pressed both hands under the dirt, feeling and feeding and taking. The ground beneath them shook as the seedlings rooted deep while splitting the soil around them pulsing and growing. Stalks sprung upward. Leaves unfurled and blossoms popped open as if greeting the world with a great yawn.

She held back as the first fruits began to bud on the vines. This they needed to do on their own. It was necessary that the men learned to tend to the crops themselves.

Jak withdrew her hands and breathed deep. The smell of fresh greenery permeated the air. She laughed as she ran her fingers over the long leaves of a cornstalk. No matter how many times she used her magick to grow things, she still never got a bigger thrill out of anything else she did.

Stefan held his hand out to her and pulled her to her feet. "How'd we do?"

She stood close to him, his body's warmth flowing into her. "Well."

In the moonlight he looked down at her, so strong and yet so vulnerable. He'd come to her in humility asking for her forgiveness and her help. Something no man had ever done before.

Though she'd been in Luften less than a week, she

already felt more useful and at home than she had in her twenty plus years down on the ground.

Without thinking she reached out and hugged Stefan. He stiffened for a moment before relaxing and wrapping his strong arms around her. Again, a sense of peace fell over her. She rested her head on his chest and overlooked the field, allowing her body to melt into his. To Jak it felt as if she were made to be there, in his large arms. The last days she'd spent without him, the loneliness and outcast feelings she'd had back in Fairelle had seeped back into her. The thoughts of doubt and worthlessness had plagued her. Only reading had given her a reprieve from the despair that she'd become so accustomed to in Fairelle. A feeling she'd prayed she'd never feel again.

The moon hung round in the sky. Bigger and brighter than she'd seen before. The stars appeared close enough for her to reach out and touch.

"The heavens are so much bigger and brighter up here."

"I wouldn't know."

"Down on Fairelle the stars are like small twinkling lights far above us. But here they're more like enlarged candles flickering on the roof."

They stood in the dark holding each other and looking up at the sky.

"When I was a boy my mother used to bring Ivan and myself out here and look up at the sky and make up pictures in them and stories to go with the pictures. Like that star." He pointed to a large bright one right above them. "She used to say that was the Straight Up star. That if you jumped far enough and high enough someday you could catch it and then we would never need to build another candle again, because it would shine so brightly."

Jak smiled. "Did you spend much time with you mother when you were younger?"

"Some. More than we did after my sisters were born. Something changed in her when they were born. She grew distant and frustrated with my father. She became no longer content to have things stay the way they did. She wanted more for her daughters; better. Not that I blame her. I adored my little sisters and agreed that they deserved more than to just be wives and take care of houses."

"Did you ever voice this to your father?"

"Many times, but he would not listen. In the end it was his stubbornness that caused my mother and sisters to leave."

"Do you know where they are? Your sisters?"

"I assume my mother went back to her birth kingdom. Her brother was a strong man, he would have readily taken in my mother and my beautiful sisters using both their strength and beauty to more firmly secure his throne."

Jak's gut clenched to think of Stefan's sisters being used as pawns in their uncle's game of power. Not much unlike her plight with her own father. Perchance it was the lot of women to be seen and used as men thought fitting. But not her. She would rather die alone and in the gutter than be a pawn for men to use as they pleased.

Stefan rested his cheek on the top of her head. "I won't let that happen to you Jak. I would lay down my life to see you happy and free rather than be treated like goods to be bartered and sold for someone else's gain."

Jak bit her lip. Her heartbeat fluttered and her chest tightened as words she wanted to say danced on her lips. "I wasn't pushing you away the other night," she said quickly. "I mean, I did push you away but... it wasn't for why you think."

"Then why did you?"

Dammit. Why couldn't she just keep quiet? Let the words go unspoken? Why did she always have to open her big mouth?

She breathed in deeply. There was no turning back now. She'd spoken up, now she needed to spill out all of her truths. No matter how silly he thought her afterward. "Because I was afraid. I am inexperienced, and I feared I would be displeasing or be too small."

Stefan's chuckle rumbled in his chest. "And just what did you think would happen that night?"

Embarrassment flushed her skin. What had she expected to happen a few nights past? Had she expected him to throw her on the bed and ravish her? Had she expected him to declare his love for her and beg her to stay and be his bride? It all seemed so silly now that she thought of it.

"I... I was not sure. I only knew I was confused and afraid."

He tipped her chin forcing her gaze to meet his. "I would never see you be afraid of me. And as for displeasing me, there are very few things you could do that would displease me. And none of them involve being intimate. Besides, how many women do you suspect me of having lain with?"

She shrugged as jealousy rooted deep in her breast. "I'm sure I know not." *I'm sure I don't want to know, either.*

He pushed a strand of hair behind her ear. "I promise you even fewer than you might think."

"But you are the prince. Handsome, strong, brave…"

His knuckles caressed her cheek. "I'm glad you think me so."

They stared into each other's eyes for a long minute. The sounds of insects chirping met Jak's ears for the first time. A slight breeze ruffled Stefan's hair and brought with it the scent of the vegetable plants she had recently helped to flourish. In that spot, in that moment, she'd never felt more happiness in her life. If she went back to Fairelle, she would remember that time in his arms, under the canopy of stars forever.

"You told me the other night that the words I'd said to you were the kindest a man has ever spoken. Did you not have many suitors on the low ground?" Stefan asked.

"I had men look at me, stare at me. Some with fear. Some with lust. But all of them like the one who wanted to marry me. Not for love, or kindness, but out of the need to possess. The desire to own. To dominate. The one who traded for me was worst of all. A year ago he'd been nothing more than a thug. Making this and that, selling it for nothing and barely making a wage. Cheating and gambling wherever he could. Stealing and…" An idea whispered through Jak's mind. *Stealing. A thief…* Was it possible?

"What is it?"

"The thief. The one who's been stealing from you. Did

he take..." Her stomach tied into a knot. "A hair comb? Purple and pink jeweled with a butterfly on it?"

"It was my mother's. The twin is still in my brother Ivan's room. But how did you know that?"

Jak's jaw clenched as a memory of Rupert, smug and cocky sitting at the gambling table at the inn floated back to her. "The man who wanted to marry me offered me one before I left." She shook her head. "I knew it wasn't right how he suddenly came upon so much wealth."

"You know the man who stabbed my father." An edge had crept into Stefan's voice. One of anger and urgency. "When the beanstalk returns. I think it might finally be time to visit the low ground."

Jak squeezed Stefan tight. "I don't want to see you hurt."

He kissed her forehead. "It isn't I that you should worry for, dear one. Only those who have done this terrible evil."

Stefan and Jak walked back through the village yard hand in hand and headed for the steps to the keep. She didn't know how much time they had spent looking at the stars and speaking of this and that, she only knew how that time had made her feel. Important, loved, seen.

No man had ever asked her questions before the way Stefan had. He'd asked her about her village. About Rupert too, but more than that. He'd asked about her life. Her upbringing. Where and when she'd discovered her powers. How she had learned to control them. He'd been in awe of her when she'd informed him that just like learning to read and write she'd had to teach herself how to use her magickal abilities.

He'd told her of the plans he had for the kingdom. The ways in which he wanted to improve the drainage from the animal pens. The arena he wanted to build for Pasha and the others. They'd discussed ways to shore up the crumbling walls around the kingdom and rebuilding the large stone gate at the front. She'd suggested capturing the large wild fowl in the forest to use as a food source. About building a pen for them and nests so they could breed. They'd even come up with a way to transfer water more easily from the well to the keep.

Stefan helped her up the enormous steps and in her long gown she was grateful for his assistance.

The moment they stepped through the castle doors Stefan stopped. Men milled about and whispered, staring at him as he entered.

"Highness!" Clive came running down the stairs. "Highness, we've been looking for you."

Stefan strode toward him. "Where's Ivan? I must speak to him."

Clive glanced around nervously. "He's... he's upstairs with your father."

"Is he awake?" Jak could scarcely make the words come out of her mouth.

"I'm so sorry." Clive's gaze traveled to Jak and then back to Stefan. "He passed an hour ago."

CHAPTER TEN

J ak tried to not let the shaking show as she ascended the stairs with Stefan, all eyes upon them.

She hurried down the hallway struggling to keep up with Stefan as he all but ran to his father's chamber. Outside stood several men, their expressions grim but Stefan ignored them. Opening the door, he strode inside and stopped so suddenly Jak almost ran into him.

Ivan stood off to the side, relaxed for the first time since Jak had met him. His gaze traveled to her, and he inclined his head making a chill run through her. Was he being nice to her? If that was so, he must indeed be in pain. Jak returned his nod and then focused on Stefan, her heart going out to him.

Stefan knelt by the bed and took his father's hand. He bowed his head and sat for several minutes. Jak tried not to shuffle from foot to foot but the longer she stood, the more she felt like this was something Stefan needed to deal with on his own. She wanted to touch him and lend her support, but she grew acutely aware that it was not her place.

She glanced at Ivan, who stared at his father and brother, a mask of unreadable emotion planted on his face.

Jak backed up slowly, step by step, until she hit the chamber door. She turned the handle and slipped out, allowing the men their time with their father.

Whispers abounded as she headed to Stefan's rooms.

"What will we do now?"

"Will Stefan take over?"

"I won't stay under Ivan's rule if Stefan doesn't step up."

Jak swallowed hard and headed into her room. She closed the door and leaned against it. Poor Stefan. Even for all of his father's faults, she knew that Stefan loved his father dearly. The blow of losing him was bound to do one of two things, crush him in pain or help him to learn to stand on his own and do what is needed.

Moments passed and the silence stretched out. She wondered what she would feel when her own father passed. Would she even mourn his loss?

No longer able to stand her own thoughts Jak walked around and tidied the room. She straightened Stefan's bed and fluffed his pillows. She picked up his clothing, folded it, and put things away. Next, she straightened the paper scattered on his table, reshelved his books, and finally swept the floor and started a fire in the fireplace, and then sat next to it, poking at the timber and ashes and allowing her thoughts to wander.

AN HOUR LATER STEFAN SLUMPED INTO HIS ROOM, shoulders bent from the weight of everything that lay before him now that his father lay dead. Jak hopped to her feet and they stared at each other for a moment before she pulled out a chair at his table for him. His feet moved as if from their own accord, and he plopped into the chair.

Jak reached for him, but then pulled away. "Are you hungry?"

"No thank you." His voice barely came out above a whisper. More than anything he wanted to hold her. To feel her delicate warm body pressed into his. To have her hands cradle his face while her soft lips kissed away the pain.

"Water? Or mead perhaps?"

He shook his head.

Every fiber of him wanted to grab onto her. To weep on her shoulder and hear words of comfort pour from her lips. But he didn't want to lay his burdens on her. She had enough on her platter without him adding to it.

"If...you don't need me, I can head to bed and leave you to your thoughts." She turned toward her room but Stefan reached out and caught her hand.

"Would you read to me?" he asked.

"Yes. Of course." She gave him a sad smile and squeezed his hand before going to the bookshelf and retrieving a book.

Jak returned to the table and sat in the chair next to him. He didn't speak. Didn't question what book it was. Didn't look at her. He merely stared into the fire, as pain and anger and fear mixed inside him like a magickal brew.

Jak opened the book and read for over an hour. Page

after page. Word after word. Her lilting voice floated through the room weaving a tale of happiness and love.

When she finally paused to take a breath Stefan's hand landed lightly on hers.

"Thank you," he said. "Thank you for everything. For trying to help him. For helping us tonight. For this."

She looked deep into his eyes and he could see her struggling for words. The expression of empathy and kindness had his tears ready to spill. Stefan couldn't afford for her to see him so low. Now more than ever he needed those around him to see his strength and leadership. He needed them to know he was ready and able to take charge and help heal his people.

He stood, his gaze not meeting hers, and kissed her on the top of her head. He breathed in the scent of her hair. "I think I'll go to bed now." He didn't wait for a reply before going to his bed and falling onto it.

He lay staring at the ceiling, willing the numbness that had entered him to consume him and push him past the barrier to slumber.

A moment passed and then Jak's chair scraped across the floor as she stood. Stefan heard the small patter of her footsteps as she went to the bookcase and replaced the book. Then she crossed to his bed, tugged off his boots and set them next to his nightstand.

She walked silently to her bedroom door, stepped inside her room and closed the door behind her.

Stefan's eyes squeezed tight as tears leaked from his sockets.

The following morning Jak awoke to Stefan moving around in his room. She slipped from her bed and opened the door that separated them. He pulled a tunic over his immensely muscular chest and turned to see her.

"Morning."

She gave him a tight smile and pushed her hair from her still sleep-soaked eyes. "Good morning."

He sat on his bed and pulled on his boots. "I must get down to the men and start them working for the day."

"Stefan—"

"If you would like to help you are welcome, but in no way obligated."

She took a step forward. "Stefan—"

"The food is running low in the stores, but hopefully since the animals are now in pens, it should be easier to collect. If you give me an hour—"

"Stefan!"

He stopped moving but didn't look up from his boots. Jak crossed to him and placed her hands on his broad shoulders. He finally lifted his gaze. His eyes red from tears. Bags puffed beneath them. She put her hand on his cheek and cupped it with her palm.

"You should take the day for yourself. Mourn properly. Spend time with your brother."

He placed his hand atop hers and then pulled it from his face. "I wish I had the time to do those things, but today is not that day. Today I need to show the men what I intend on doing with our kingdom. The things you and I discussed under the stars. I need to convince them that Luften is the place they want to be. The place they want to rebuild a life. I can't do that if I lay in my bed like a child and drown my sorrows in ale and tears."

Jak gripped his hand tightly. "Then let me get dressed, and I shall help you."

"Jak—"

"Do you think I wish to sit around all day and do nothing? I've been going crazy for the past three days in this place with nothing to do. Either you let me help, or I am afraid you might return this evening to find I've rearranged all the furniture in the castle."

He gave her a gentle smile. "All right."

THE DAY FLEW BY AS SIDE-BY-SIDE JAK, STEFAN, AND surprisingly Ivan, got the men to work. Jak spent the day telling the men what they needed to do to keep the crops growing. She instructed the men on both where and when individual seeds should be planted. She showed the men how to mend their clothing and how to cook several simple meals out of the food which remained. Finally, she taught them how to grind the grain into flour and make bread.

Stefan and Ivan kept the men to task shoring up the village walls, fixing their roofs and huts, tilling more area to plant and burning everything ruined or no longer of use.

By the time evening arrived there was fresh bread and stew for everyone. Jak sat with the men in a circle around the bonfire of trash listening to them joke, tell stories and laugh. So much about their countenances as well as the kingdom itself had changed since her arrival. But more so since the news of the death of the king.

"This is all your fault you know." Ivan sat next to her.

Jak's smile faded and she looked up at him sideways. "Oh? How so?"

Ivan shrugged. "You gave Stefan a purpose. A reason to change. A need to want to make things better. And because of that, the men are changing. I hadn't heard a laugh in the kingdom in months before you arrived."

Jak picked at her bread. "And you think this because of me?"

Ivan looked down at her. "I know it is."

Her cheeks flushed with heat, and she looked over to where Stefan talked with several men.

"Then, I'm sure you are patting yourself on the back right now, aren't you?"

His eyebrows raised bringing a youthful appearance to his rugged face. "I haven't done anything."

"Nothing but bring me here."

Their gazes connected and he gave her a lopsided grin. "I'd like to tell you I feel bad for having done so, but with all that's transpired I am afraid I would be lying."

"Well," she said. "If you cannot apologize for what you did, perhaps you can do me a favor instead."

His eyes narrowed. "And what is that?"

"From here on out you can promise there will never be lies between us. No deceit. We will be honest and truthful. And in the future, if you need something, ask. I am much more amenable when asked for help instead of forced."

Ivan chuckled. A low, rumbly sound that she was sure hadn't been heard from him in a long while.

"That I can do," he replied.

A man pulled out a harmonica and began to play. One by one, Jätte stood and began to dance. A second man pulled out two metal spoons and tapped them along in rhythm. The men clapped, laughed and danced around the fire.

Jak smiled to herself.

A hand appeared in front of her. She cocked an eyebrow.

"Would you care to dance?" Ivan asked.

She snorted. "Do you know how?"

He broke into a broad smile identical to Stefan's. "Believe it or not, I can actually move my feet."

She slipped her hand into his. "That I'd like to see."

Ivan pulled her to her feet and whirled her in a circle. Jak laughed as she and Ivan rounded the fire. The men clapped and cheered as she was lifted and spun and twirled and pulled around by Ivan. After several minutes she jerked her hand away, breathing hard.

"I concede," she breathed. "You can dance."

Ivan laughed. "I am not the villain you think I am. I do possess some decent qualities."

She nodded. "A few perhaps."

Stefan stepped up and held his hand out to her. "May I cut in?"

Ivan slapped his brother on the shoulder. "She's all yours."

The music and rhythm slowed, and Stefan pulled her

close to him. His arm slipped around her waist like a thick tree branch, and she slid her hand up his forearm. They swayed to the music as they danced around the group.

"I see you and Ivan have made up."

"Came to an understanding, more like."

"I can never thank you for what you've done. Nothing I say will ever be enough to express my gratitude."

"All I ask is that you don't stop. Whatever it takes, you finish what you started. Don't let the memory of your father drown you in guilt for rebuilding and doing what you know is right."

He watched her for a long moment. "What do you want Jak?"

"What?"

"You. What do you want? All this time you've given and given and given to me, to my kingdom, to my men and you've asked for nothing in return. What is the one thing you desire above all else? Tell me, and if it is within my reach, I shall give it to you."

Jak looked around as Stefan twirled her in a circle.

"This. This is what I want. A place to belong. A place to call home. A place with people I love and who love me. People willing to sacrifice for each other. To do the hard things for the sake of the love they share. I want... a home."

Stefan stopped moving. He took Jak's hand and led her away from the group.

"Come. I want to show you something."

Stefan pulled Jak up the steps of the castle and through the front doors. Without a word he led her up to the top floor and down past his rooms to the end of the hallway. In the corner stood a plain wooden door. He pulled her through it and up the narrow winding staircase.

Her eyes widened as she took in the spacious room.

"Mother used to tutor us here when we were young. After she stopped, I used it as a room for myself. I used to come up here to think or to listen to music or to read. But mostly I came up here at night to do something else."

He took her hand and led her over to an open window. In front stood a telescope. He pulled a chair over for her to stand on and positioned the telescope for her to see through.

"I often stand here and watch the stars but more than that I love to stand here and look out over our lands." He pushed the telescope to the right. "Over there is the forest we visited." He tipped it up a bit. "Beyond is a waterfall where I used to swim with Ivan and my father." He moved the telescope again. "That is where we used to hold the spring festival. There were axe throwing contests. Baking contests. Dancing. Singing. Everyone looked forward to it all year."

Jak pulled her eyes from the telescope. "You will celebrate again."

He nodded. His chest tightened at the words he wanted to say. The words that would open him up to possibly the most considerable crushing pain of his lifetime. He paused. If she rejected him, he didn't know if he could handle it right then. Yet at the same time not speaking his heart was just as painful.

"You can have it all," he finally said.

Her eyebrows pressed together.

"This place. You can have it as your own. You could stay here. Make it your home."

"Home?"

"You said you have nothing down on the ground. No one you call family. But here you've earned the respect of my entire kingdom. You've won over my brother, and you've... won over me as well."

"Are... are you asking me to stay?" He couldn't help but see the conflict in her eyes. The hope as well as the fear.

"Do you want to stay?" He wanted her to say yes more than anything. To have her in his life day in and day out. By his side. Brightening his existence and making it seem meaningful.

She turned and gazed out the window. "I've felt more at home here in the last week than anywhere in my lifetime. But my father—"

Anger rushed through Stefan at the mention of her father. A grown man whom she had been forced to tend to and look after as if a small child. "Your father needs to stand on his own two feet. He can no longer use you as a crutch or a punching bag. You need to let him succeed or fail on his own. You aren't his caretaker, you are his daughter. Hell, a mother wouldn't do so much as you have."

Jak stared silently out the window for several minutes. "I should like to see that waterfall with you and swim in its pool. To find my mother tree and meet her. To explore the forest and discover all of the strange animals. To be here for your spring celebration and watch your men laugh and have fun. I would enjoy seeing the plants bear fruit and come to harvest."

He placed his hand on hers.

"But..."

He didn't want to rush her. Their gazes met and he leaned in and brushed her soft lips with his. She squeezed his hand tightly and a crash of desire washed over him. He leaned his forehead on hers. "Don't answer now. There are several more days until the stalk returns. Think on my offer. Make a decision for yourself for once. Do not think on what others may want or need. Think only of what your heart wants."

She nodded and then returned her eye to the telescope. Stefan watched as she moved the large instrument with her petite hands and then settled on something in the distance.

"What are those?" she asked.

"What?" Stefan looked out the window to where the telescope pointed. Small light dots scattered across the landscape.

Jak moved so he could see through the telescope. "Those lights. Do you see them?"

Stefan's heartbeat quickened. Dozens of lights flickered across the fields several leagues off. His blood chilled. Lights and tents, and men amassed less than two hours from the village gates.

"Stefan?"

"If I'm right, that's an army."

"An army? But surely they cannot have heard of your father's death already?"

"It doesn't matter. By morning they will be upon us, and

we aren't prepared. The walls are barely holding around the village. Our weapons haven't been used in ages. The men are more likely to fall on their swords and hurt themselves than they are to hurt someone else."

Jak's expression hardened and she squeezed his arm tightly. "Then you'll just have to get them ready."

She was the strength he'd always needed. The courage that mustered the brave. How such a tiny person could exude such a large presence, he would never know.

Stefan nodded. "We need to find Ivan."

CHAPTER ELEVEN

Ivan folded his arms over his chest. "What kind of problem?"

"There's an army camped across the fields. I believe they intend on attacking at first light."

"How could they have heard about father's death so quickly?"

Stefan shook his head. "I don't think that's it. When Jak and I went to the forest to find the fernblend, two Jätte tried to kidnap Pasha. We fought. One of them may have said he was a prince or something."

Ivan took a step forward. "And you are only now telling me about this?"

"They seemed nothing more than a couple of common thugs."

"In our lands. You should have told me." Ivan threw his hands over his face and then pulled on his hair, swearing loudly.

Stefan didn't want to argue. "You're right, but there were more important things going on at the time."

Ivan paced the room. "So now what? There is no way we can win a war. Not with how everything is in disrepair. The men have barely worked in the last few years. And I've only gotten a handful out to train in the past six months. We'll be slaughtered."

Stefan had been wracking his brain for an idea for close to an hour and he'd only come up with one that made any sense. "Maybe it's best we surrender."

"Surrender?" Ivan stopped moving. "Surrender is sure to guarantee our deaths or our slavery. Is that better?"

Stefan fought to keep his voice even. "Fighting could get everyone killed."

"You sound like father. I thought you'd decided to make up your own mind on things. Our men have been planting and fixing the kingdom. They want to save their home, and if given a choice they would fight. Father did not believe in war. Heavens knows I don't want to fight any more than you do but when tyranny is brought to our doorstep what is wrong with keeping tyranny at bay?"

Stefan shook his head. "That's how things started with grandfather. Trying to keep invaders out. Soon he became the one that others died to keep out."

"You are not Grandfather or Father. Nor am I. We are our own men."

Jak stepped forward. "You've been fighting to bring your men back from the brink. To give them hope. To see them succeed. If you roll over now, you will be telling them you would rather see them imprisoned, enslaved or dead than raise your hand to protect them."

Wonderful, now he had to fight on two fronts. "Jak. This *is* about protecting them. You've seen them out there working and toiling. At the end of the day, they are so exhausted they can scarcely lift a spoon. How do you expect them to lift axes and hammers and spears to fight?" Stefan stepped to her and touched her arm.

She pulled away. "If you do nothing to defend Luften you are telling both the men and myself that our work, though only for a few days, is nothing and the hope you gave is false."

Stefan opened his mouth but then turned away and stared into the fireplace. He had no idea what to do. He didn't want to roll over, but neither did he want war. Either outcome would end in the death of his men.

Jak stormed from the room, her swearing making Ivan chuckle.

"I think there were a few new ones in there even I haven't heard before." He turned to Stefan and his expression sobered instantly. "You need to tell the men. Give them a choice. Let them decide what they want to do."

"And if they decide not to fight?" Stefan asked not moving from where he stared into the fire.

"Then I alone shall stand at the gate tomorrow morning and meet the oncoming horde."

Stefan finally turned to his younger brother, but like Jak had moments before, Ivan strode from the room, slamming the door behind him.

JAK HIT THE ENTRANCE JUST AS HEAVY FOOTSTEPS RAN DOWN the stairs behind her. She turned as someone jumped the last set of stairs and landed beside her. Ivan. She opened her mouth to tell him to get lost, but he held up his hand.

"What can I do to help?" He glanced over his shoulder and then placed his hand on her lower back and ushered her out the door.

"Whatever you have planned we need to hurry because I don't know what Stefan will do."

"What about you?"

"If what you plan involves protecting this kingdom and not surrendering like cowards, I am with you."

Jak bit her lip. What did she plan to do? She wracked her brain… "I need a satchel."

"Done."

She swallowed down her terror as she asked the next question. "Can you ride Pasha?"

Ivan smiled. "Of course."

"I was afraid you might say that. Come on. I have an idea," said Jak.

The pair raced down the steps and into the courtyard. They had less than eight hours before the sun rose.

THE TAKEOFF WAS JUST AS BAD AS IT HAD BEEN BEFORE, BUT this time the fear tapered off quicker. Ivan didn't offer to hold on to her and Jak didn't ask him to. He trusted her, and she had no intention of showing weakness.

They flew toward the forest twice as fast as before, and soon they were descending.

"Pasha wonders if he should land in the same place as before."

"Yes," she replied.

They swooped down toward the trees, and she held her breath until Pasha's feet hit the ground. Her heart galloped like a stampede of horses, and she slid shakily to the forest floor. Riding with Stefan had been much more enjoyable. And she'd enjoyed that not at all.

Ivan grabbed her arm as her legs buckled.

"Are you all right?"

"I don't think I will ever get used to riding a flying horse."

"Neither will I."

Ivan broke into a grin. She laughed, and he did as well.

"Finally," she said. "We have something in common."

Ivan took in their surroundings. "So, what are we doing here?"

"I need to collect some seeds."

"Seeds?"

Jak marched to the first tree and laid her hand on it. She sensed the life inside, and when it awoke, she asked the tree something she never thought she would ask before.

"Where is my mother tree?" she whispered.

The tree vibrated with energy and a whisper snaked through her mind. Nothing she could pinpoint. It wasn't words, more a feeling pulling her in a specific direction.

Jak followed the voice as it lured her forward, like a ribbon attached to her belly button. She moved her feet, unsure of where she headed, only letting herself feel the way through the forest to her destination. On and on she made her way, touching the trees as she passed, hearing their greetings in hushed, reverent tones both welcoming and thanking her at the same time. The further she hiked the more peaceful she became. Finally, only the sound of her footsteps and that of Ivan's behind her could be heard on the soft moss as they made their way through the thickest part of the forest. Jak squeezed through a pair of trees and stopped. She turned to Ivan.

"Wait here."

He nodded.

Jak pushed through the thick brush and found herself face to face with a giant wall of vines. They grew higher than she could see and when she tried to slip between them, she got her entire arm inside and could still feel more on her fingertips.

She drew her hand back and took in the immensity of the vine wall. Whatever it protected had to be of great value.

Jak swallowed hard as the ribbon pulled her toward the vines. This was it. Beyond stood her mother tree, its life pulsed through her veins.

"I can't see you anymore," Ivan called.

"I'll be back shortly," she replied.

"Hurry. This place is creeping me out."

Jak laid her palms on the vines. They shook but did not move. She opened her mind to them and let them feel her magic. For several seconds nothing happened. Then, like the unraveling of a knit scarf, the vines untangled themselves and created a pathway big enough for her to fit through.

As Jak wedged through the vines they reached out and touched her, stroking her arms and legs and feet as if trying to catch a piece of her essence. The path continued for several yards. As she neared the end a faint violet light greeted her.

Jak emerged from the vine hedge into the most beautiful place she'd ever seen. A vibrant violet pool trickled water on one side of the glade. Tall iridescent flowers swayed to a light breeze smelling of fruit and honey. An array of birds and other animals she'd never seen before sat in the trees gawking at her. A giant cat, black with light spots stared at her from the limb of a tree, it's tail swishing back and forth. An animal much larger and fiercer looking than the little apinas swayed from foot to foot and called to her like the hooting of an owl. A snake the length of her hut slithered over her foot, its tongue probing the air for information. And a unicorn, its horn like a beautiful opal, pranced across the green and into a cave behind the waterfall.

Fireflies and luminary butterflies floated around giving a golden glow to the place. Finally, in the middle of the meadow, like a proud warrior, stood an enormous white tree with golden fruit hanging from its limbs. Warmth spread through Jak as if she'd suddenly sunk into a tub of bathwater.

"Hello, Jakleen."

A tall, willowy figure floated out of the enormous tree. She was more than a good head taller than Jak, but bore the same fair skin with aqua hair and bright seafoam eyes. She floated toward Jak like an ethereal image and stopped several feet away.

The two stared at each other for several moments.

The woman nodded. "I am Yesenia, Queen of the Forests."

So many questions burst into Jak's mind. "You are my mother."

"I am glad you finally found your way here. You must have so many questions." Yesenia floated to a jutting rock near the pool and sat down.

Jak continued to stare for a moment more. "You're dead, aren't you?"

"I am neither dead nor undead. I am a spirit. The spirit of the Illumis tree."

"But you have no form? No body."

"We are allowed a body from time to time in which we can procreate and bring about new life if we wish."

"You mean produce children. Are there more like me?"

"You are my only offspring." Yesenia dipped her hand in the water. It swirled around her fingers and sent ripples across the pool. "You wonder why I left you with your human father and did not raise you myself, but that isn't your most pressing concern, is it?" Yesenia looked up at her again.

Jak knew in her gut whatever answers she got they would not be satisfactory.

"I need seeds for the vines protecting this glade as well as for trees."

Yesenia stared at her for a long moment. "Are you intending on raising a forest to put your own tree into?"

Her own tree? She could have her own tree? "No. To protect Luften."

Yesenia's eyebrows raised. "Luften?"

"They are going to be wiped out if they don't get help. I need the seeds, so I can grow protection around them."

"You wish the trees to fight for you."

"I wish for them to protect."

Again, her mother stared at the water. "I must say, this is not what I'd expected."

"And what had you expected? A daughter so grief-stricken for the mother she'd never known that she would go off on a grand adventure to search you out and come learn at your knee about who she is?"

The answer rang from Yesenia's eyes.

"I'm sorry to disappoint, but if you'd wanted a daughter like that maybe you should have never left her with a drunken gambler in the first place. Do you want to know what my life was like down there on the low ground? How I played maid and cook and housekeeper to a man who left me hungry and cold more than he did fed and in warmth? Or how in all of my life I've never had a kind word from him or any other human in the village. Or how right before being kidnapped and brought up here he sold me off in a hand of cards to a man no better than he. All so he could pay off some debt and keep the drinks flowing at the tavern."

"I wanted you to learn what it was like to be human."

"Why? So, I could learn cruelty and mockery, debauchery and shame? Yes, there are decent people in the world down there. But not where you left me."

Silence hung thick in the air between them, only cut by the sounds of frogs the size of dinner plates croaking on the bank of the pond.

"If you want the trees help, you need to ask them yourself. I cannot give you anything; neither are you allowed to take, but that which they give you freely you are welcome to."

The ribbon that had pulled Jak into the grove now pulled her toward the immense white Illumis tree.

Yesenia sat silently as Jak passed her.

The tree pulsed with life. As she laid her hand upon it, she could hear and feel every single tree in the glade. Every bird. Every creature. Every flower. All of them, connected to the tree. The tree reached out and sucked her body flat against it. Like a mother's embrace, the tree held her close and soothed her pain. Tears fell from Jak's eyes as an overabundance of love flooded into her.

Every tree and plant infiltrated her and all at once she gained a lifeline to each of them. In a flash, all thoughts and desires floated from her and whispered throughout the meadow. The Illumis tree shook and Jak stepped away. One if its branches stretched down to her and she held out her hands as a piece of fruit dropped into her palms. Like a rainstorm, the trees and plants around her shook and bore their fruits and seeds to the ground as well.

Jak took in the plethora of life and then sprinted to the different trees gathering as many of the nuts and seeds as she could carry.

Yesenia strolled through the garden touching each of the

plants in turn, bowing her head and speaking to them in hushed tones.

Jak wanted to say something, but had no words. There would be time enough to come back after everything had settled in Luften. She headed back to the path in the vines.

"You understand what it means don't you?"

Jak turned.

"That the Illumis tree has given you a fruit?" her mother asked.

Jak inspected the golden fruit in her hand. Was she supposed to eat it?

"The Illumis tree chose you as the guardian for its offspring. It only ever picks one. With that fruit you will grow your own Illumis tree. A tree from which all of your knowledge and power will spring. If it is ever cut down, you will wither and die as will all life in your forest to which it is connected. You must eat the fruit and plant the seeds. After, the two of you will be forever bound to each other. I suggest you not do that unless you are truly ready to become the guardian of your tree."

Jak cradled the fruit in her palm. "Then I shall care for it as if it was my own child."

Yesenia's eyes belied the fact that she'd caught Jak's jab at her.

"Perhaps you will come to see me again when you have more time." The sadness that crossed her mother's face was unmistakable.

"I will return." Jak strode to the hedge and then stopped. "Thank you... mother." Instead of turning Jak continued on through the vines and back toward the place she planned on saving.

"THANK THE SKIES YOU CAME BACK. FOR A MINUTE I WAS afraid I was going to have to try and force my way in wherever it was you went." Ivan stepped forward and helped her through the vines. "Did you get what you wanted?"

"No. But I got what I needed."

Together they raced to Pasha and this time when they took off, Jak was too preoccupied to notice.

Pasha flew faster than ever, and by the time they'd landed Jak knew what she needed to do.

"I need you to gather as many Jätte as you think can keep quiet." She dismounted. "I am going to need several bowls and a space to work in unhindered."

Ivan nodded. "In the back of the stable is a tack room. It has never been used, so it should be fairly cleaned out. I'm going to need to prepare the men. They have to be warned."

Jak nodded and followed Pasha into the stable as Ivan ran the other direction. They walked halfway down when Pasha nodded his head toward the wall. She spotted what he motioned to. A lantern hung on a hook and next to it sat a flint and tinder.

"Thank you," she said. She lit the lamp and headed toward the back of the stable. Pasha trotted into his stall as Jak continued to the room beyond.

A thick layer of dust settled over the room. The walls were lined with tools and bridles and other items, but in the middle sat a sturdy table with chairs. She set the satchel on top of it. Turning up the lantern she hung it on the wall. She found two more lanterns and had just finished lighting them when Ivan arrived with several men. They crowded into the room where they each took a seat at the table.

Ivan handed her the bowls and Jak spread them out on the table. She took her satchel and turned it over. The seeds, nuts, and golden fruit tumbled out.

"Whoa." One of the Jätte reached for the fruit, but Jak snatched it up, put it back in her satchel and slung it over her shoulder.

"That's not for you," she said.

The Jätte turned to Ivan who folded his arms over his chest, giving the man a grim expression.

"All right," said Jak. "I am going to separate the seeds and nuts, and then I am going to need your help placing them around Luften."

"That would take days to separate all of these," said a man.

"For you perhaps." Jak raised her hands. She identified each seed by their kind and pushed them into separate bowls. The vines into one. Trees into another. Flowers and ground covers into a third.

After several minutes she opened her eyes, and they were all where she wanted them.

The Jätte stared at her with a mixture of fear and wonder.

She picked up the bowl with the vine seeds and handed it to Ivan. "These need to be spread outside the walls and inside. They only need to be dropped one at a time, not in handfuls, but we need to surround the walls inside and out."

Ivan nodded.

She retrieved the bowl with the tree nuts. "These should be placed six to eight feet apart on the outside of the walls only. We don't want crowding."

She handed the nuts to the man who'd reached for the golden fruit.

"You, Rudis and Miller do that bowl," said Ivan.

The three men got up and headed out.

"Lastly," Jak added. "This bowl needs to be distributed on the top of each of the huts. Again, you don't need a lot, but each roof needs them."

Ivan nodded to three other men. They took the bowl and left as well.

"Are you sure this will work?"

"I am sure I can do my part if that's what you are asking. What happens in the morning is up to you and Stefan. But I will do what I can to protect Luften, as well as Pasha and the others."

"We'll get this done."

"Hurry. This is going to take a while to finish."

Ivan strode from the room with the remaining men, and Jak plopped into the hard wooden chair. She sat the satchel on the table again and pulled out the golden fruit. She rolled the oblong fruit in her hands, staring at its golden skin. She'd met her mother and had gotten her own fruit to grow an Illumis tree. The question was, where would she plant it and was she ready?

CHAPTER TWELVE

S tefan spent an hour and a half trying to convince himself to take up arms and let the men fight, but he knew doing so would be the death of all of them. If he could perhaps make a deal with the other kingdom...

Stefan yelled in frustration and pulled at his hair. The very thought was futile. If they were the men from the forest, there would be no reasoning with them.

He'd stomped to his chamber and threw himself on his bed and stared at the ceiling for at least another hour trying to figure a way out of their current situation. He didn't want to be a coward like his father, nor could he afford to rush in and risk lives the way his grandfather had. For the first time in years he wished his mother was there to give her council. For all of her faults, she had always had a good head for battle.

Stefan glanced at the clock and his eyebrows scrunched together. He looked to Jak's door which stood open and her room empty. She'd been absent for several hours at least. A gnawing at his gut made him want to search her out, but he wasn't ready to hear her opinions at the moment.

Her anger with him for not rushing into a fight surprised him, though honestly it shouldn't have. From what she'd told him of her life it sounded like she'd had to fight for everything she'd gotten. Even more surprising had been her taking the same stance as Ivan on the subject. He couldn't deny the jealousy that had scoured through him the night before when he'd caught the two of them speaking at the bonfire and then when Ivan had lifted Jak in the air and danced with her, it had been all he could do to keep a civil tongue with his brother. He didn't like feeling like they were keeping him out. Which he knew was stupid, but he'd become so attached to Jak in such a short period of time that the thought of losing her to another was almost enough to break him in two.

Ivan and Jak were right. He should let the men decide. But what if their decision got all of them killed? All of their blood would land at his feet, and he wasn't sure he could handle that guilt.

Making a rash decision would get them all killed for sure. He needed to think through his options. So far, he'd not been able to come up with anything himself. He needed help. Council. Even if he didn't want to hear it, even if it didn't coincide with his own desires, he needed it. And he needed it from Jak and Ivan.

· · ·

Stefan searched the castle but couldn't find them. Anxiety built inside him. No matter what happened to him, he refused to let Jak be harmed because of his and Ivan's foolishness. She'd done enough for them. He wouldn't let her fall prey to another clan.

Stefan walked toward the castle doors where several men gathered. "Have any of you seen Jak?"

The men looked from one to another.

"The tiny woman with blue hair, Jak, have you seen her?"

An uneasiness came over the group, sending Stefan's protective nature into overdrive. He rushed to the first man and grabbed his arm.

"Where is she?"

The man pointed over his shoulder. Stefan tore open the front door and ran down the castle steps. A strange creaking noise floated up from the village. The scent of grass and flowers and trees invaded him as he drew closer to the square. Men stood at the bottom of the steps staring into the night. Stefan followed their gaze, trying to make out what he saw.

He fought to take in the essence of what transpired around him. She was creating a forest. A beautiful, lush, thick, impenetrable forest all around Luften.

The walls of the village were covered in thick vines. Trees creaked and groaned as they stretched higher into the air creating a barrier around the entire village. Green grass dotted with small flowers covering the rooftops of the huts. The garden grew taller and plump ripe vegetables weighed down the different vines and stalks. The patch of green they'd planted for Pasha and his herd now stood almost knee high. It was as if he watched the gods create the world around him.

Stefan moved forward taking in the beautiful sight. Someone nudged Stefan's shoulder. Pasha stood proudly to his right looking on.

"Seems she has taken matters into her own hands."

Stefan's eyes narrowed. "Why do I feel you helped with this?"

Pasha shook his mane. *"I simply provided the ride."*

"You took her alone back to the forest? Either one of you could've been harmed or killed."

"No." Pasha nodded his head, and Stefan followed his gaze.

Jak sat on the ground in the middle of the village square and beside her, like a mountain of protection, stood Ivan.

"Ivan went with you?" A pang of shame pushed through him. Ivan had gone with Jak and done what Stefan dared not.

Stefan pressed forward and stopped at Ivan's side.

Ivan spotted him before focusing on Jak again. "I won't let you stop her."

Again, a sliver of jealousy wriggled its way through him. "What makes you think I want to stop her?"

Ivan stared at Stefan, long and hard. "So, you're prepared to fight?"

Was he? Was he willing to stand against the oncoming horde?

"I will do whatever is necessary to protect those I love."

Ivan laid his hand on Stefan's shoulder. "That's good to

hear. Because I don't think the men will follow unless you lead."

Stefan stared at Jak. "I think they've already found a leader."

Ivan chuckled. "Jak isn't a leader. She's a catalyst. And believe it or not, the men have been waiting for someone to come along and tell them to change. As much as you don't like father's old-fashioned ideas about male and female roles, it is what the men are used to. They are used to being told what to do by their wives. Changing that will take time, but in this instance, it works."

Ivan and Stefan stood for more than two hours watching Jak work. By the end of it, every man in the kingdom had gathered in the village center.

"I can't believe it," said one.

"She grew a forest," said another.

"I like it," said a third.

The men stood in awe of the beauty surrounding them. Stefan wondered if they understood the meaning. If they realized what she'd done it for. Beauty yes, but more, to protect them.

"How are we supposed to get out?" someone whispered.

"What do you care? You never leave," Ivan replied.

Silence flooded the village as the trees and grass, and vines creaked to a halt. Silence blossomed around them like a cocoon of safety as Stefan took in the new breathtaking and slightly terrifying scenery.

Jak rose from her spot and stretched. Stefan rushed forward and helped her to her feet, and she gave a tired smile.

"That took a lot more than simply growing one tree."

"Let's get you rest."

He could see she wanted to argue so without a word he swept her into his arms and headed back toward the castle.

"What should we do?" Ivan called.

"Prepare!" Stefan replied. "Prepare to defend against invaders."

"You heard the king," Ivan yelled. "Prepare to fight!"

STEFAN CARRIED JAK UP TO HIS CHAMBER, WALKED TO HIS bed, and laid her on it. Her eyelids drooped as she peered up at him.

"You've been busy."

She smiled. "A bit."

He covered her with a blanket and sat on the edge of the bed next to her.

"Sleep."

"You aren't angry with me?"

He shook his head. "I'm not angry. I just don't understand why. Why would you do this for us? After we kidnapped you, why would you help us?"

She reached out and laid her hand atop his. "I didn't help them, I helped you."

Stefan's heart shuddered as his ribcage squeezed like platemail.

"I have learned in the past days that parents are not always right just because they are your parents. You asked me to help you by growing the crops and giving your men something to fight for. I did what you requested of me. I gave you all something worth fighting for."

Stefan brushed the hair from Jak's eyes. How could a creature be so gentle, so kind, and still so fierce at the same time? She grasped his hand in hers and pressed it to her cheek.

"I like how that feels."

Stefan's body stiffened at her words, and a sudden rush of desire made his breeches tighten around his arousal.

She stared up at him, her eyes soft and full. She ran her tiny hand up his tunic making his gut quiver.

Her hand fisted in his shirt and pulled him down to her. Stefan's heart pounded. He wanted to smother her in kisses. To hold her in his arms and keep her safe. To taste her skin and run his calloused hands over every inch.

She pulled him close until his mouth waited inches from hers. He stopped, wanting her to be certain. Agonizing seconds passed, so close and yet the inches separating them seemed the distance of the universe.

"I've never done this before," she whispered.

"Are you sure you want to?"

"I... I pushed you away before because I was afraid."

"And now?"

"Now all I want is here. All I want is you."

Stefan brushed his lips against hers. She let out a soft mewl like a tiny cat. She sat up slightly and pressed her soft lips to his. The scent of soil, flowers and life clung to her as if she was made of it. Stefan pressed his mouth harder against hers, running his tongue along her bottom lip. She touched his cheek as she parted her lips and their tongues interwove.

He needed her, wanted her. All sense of reason was almost overrun by desire. Stefan broke the kiss and placed his forehead on hers taking a deep breath.

"Did I do it wrong?"

"No." He kissed her again. "No, you did it right. Very right."

"Then why did you stop?"

"Because you are tired and need to rest. We have only a few hours until the sun is up and as much as I want this, I also want you to rest and be clear-headed for when we do finally get a chance to be together."

Stefan sat up, and then rolled next to her. He pulled her into his arms and allowed his body to relax into hers as she curled into him.

"I don't understand."

He kissed the top of her head. "Now is not the right time."

She nuzzled her head in the crook of his shoulder, and he allowed the peace of the night to wash over him. Never before had he held a woman in his bed. Nor had he slept with one in his arms. His relations with woman had not been many, but the few he'd experienced were more about need, not a lasting relationship.

Stefan laid his head back and relaxed into his pillow, letting the feel and scent of Jak invade him and praying it would not be the last time he would hold her.

· · ·

STEFAN AWOKE TO THE SUN PEEKING THROUGH HIS WINDOW and a slight rap on his door. Jak continued to sleep soundly as he gently scooted out from under her.

Ivan stood on the other side. "They've been spotted marching toward Luften."

Stefan nodded. "I'll meet you downstairs."

Ivan peered over Stefan's shoulder. "You should wake her. We might need her."

Stefan shook his head. "I am locking her in. If things go south my only concern is for her safety and yours."

Ivan set his hand on Stefan's shoulder. "If things go south, you are not to think of me. You are to grab Jak and Pasha and the herd and take to the skies. Find a place to hide until the stalk returns then fly them to the ground and build a life for yourself out of harm's way."

"I'll never leave you."

"We'll see about that when the time comes. Just know that if you choose her, I agree."

Stefan's gut twisted. He'd never heard such words of love from his brother before. And he was sure he never would again.

Stefan set his hands on his brother's shoulders and then bowed his head and touched Ivan's forehead with his own. "Let us pray it doesn't come to that."

STEFAN JOGGED DOWN THE STAIRS TO THE MAIN FLOOR dropping his chamber key back inside his shirt against his chest. It'd been so long since he'd worn his armor that the feel of his pauldron dug into his shoulder as his battle-axe weighed heavier in his gloved hand. For himself, he wasn't afraid of the battle to come, but for Jak and Ivan and even his men, he feared where this conflict would end.

Ivan waited with several armed men.

"You four stay here and guard the castle. It's our last line of defense should the rest of us fall."

The men nodded. A horn sounded a long low blast from without the walls. Stefan clapped Ivan on his armored shoulder.

"'Tis time."

Ivan stepped out of the way. Stefan clutched the key at his neck and prayed to the gods to keep Jak safe as he strode down the keep steps to where the majority of his men awaited him. To call them a motley crew would be too generous. The only thing that brought hope to Stefan's breast was the determined look in their eyes and the knee that they bent to him as he passed.

The closer Stefan got to the village the more he could see all that had been done. The vines wound up the walls entwining with the rocks and giving them a more solid foundation. The trees on the other side stood like sentinels ensuring any attackers would not easily be able to use ladders or siege weapons to gain entrance. The grass on the roofs meant that any flaming arrows shot into the village would be extinguished instead of setting the huts aflame. And with Pasha and the herd no longer contained within the stable, they were now free to escape if necessary, without aid or assistance. The entire setup had been done so meticulously that Stefan could swear that Jak had done it before.

They reached the village center, and the men gathered around them.

"I speak to you as I should have to my father in years past. He set us on a course for failure the moment he refused to change. He let Luften wither and die. But as you can see, we will not be refused. We have decided change is not a bad thing. We want to live and thrive as we once did. Not by sword and pillaging, but by living our lives to the fullest. To once again be blessed with wives and children. Wives who are proud to be here and wives that we value above all else. This cannot be achieved by sitting idle. Nor can it be done by rolling over for a horde of dogs. So, I ask you, the men of Luften, with enemies once more at our gates, what do you want to do? Fight or become slaves?"

Not even a moment of pause sounded before the men cheered and joined Stefan.

"It is decided," said Ivan. "We fight!"

Stefan strode toward the front gate. "Let us go greet our guests."

CHAPTER THIRTEEN

J ak rolled over and a beam of sunlight flashed in her
eyes, making her groan and shield her face. She
snuggled deeper into the pillow that smelled of
Stefan and smiled. Her smile faded to a frown as
sleep left her and she realized where she was. She sat up.

"Stefan?"

There was no answer. Her heartbeat quickened as a
horn blew outside.

The enemy.

Jak ran to the door and pulled on the handle, but it
didn't budge.

"He did not lock me in this room."

She grasped the handle again and again it did not
budge. Jak's blood rose to the point of boiling over. Of all
the egotistical, bullheaded, male things to do. If he thought
he could lock her in to keep her from harm, he was sorely
mistaken. She marched straight to her chamber and

stormed to the window. Throwing it wide she glanced down, making her stomach lurch. *This is no time to be weak.*

Jak blew out a breath and steadied herself. *She'd* been the one to take the initiative and grow him a forest worthy of keeping out the mightiest of armies. *She* was the one who had tried to save his father. And *she* was the one who refused to be locked in a room like a fair maiden while the men went out to settle their dispute. Jak steeled her nerves and climbed onto the window ledge. She reached with her magic and the vines climbing the stone stretched for her. She grasped them as they wrapped around her wrists and ankles. Sliding out the window she clung to the rock. Using her magic, she propelled herself upward toward the roof. Foot by foot she climbed higher and higher refusing to look down or give in to her fear. When her fingers reached the roof, she grasped the stone and hauled herself up. From the top she could see everything for miles but took no time to enjoy the view. The wind whipped her hair in her face, and she stomped to the front of the castle. She spotted the army beyond the wall, and on the inside Ivan and Stefan standing upon the gate.

She wanted to call to Stefan but knew her voice would not carry that far. She needed to get down there. To help. Jak glanced around and spotted the vines running up the front of the castle. She pulled with her magic, and the vines grew and stretched up to her. Wrapping around her wrists, ankles, and waist Jak commanded them to take her down. She fought against the panic that rose in her chest as the vines lowered her to the steps outside the keep.

Set back on her feet, Jak sucked in a deep breath and

ran down the steps. Gods above she never wanted to do that again.

STEFAN STOOD UPON THE RAMPARTS OF THE GATE AND surveyed the awaiting army. The men gave way as someone moved forward and stopped at the front. The man from the forest, *Marius*. A second man stepped forward and joined the first. Though more battered and still beaten the figure was undeniably Prentis.

The groups stared at each other for a long, tense moment.

"Impressive what you've done with Luften," said Marius.

"What brings you to these lands?" Stefan called.

"I come to speak with King Julius about a grievance I bear against you." He pointed at Stefan.

"My father is dead. Anything you have to say you can say to me. But I warn you, you may not fare as well as you hope."

"I am Marius, Prince of Kinline, and you attacked me, and my man Prentis, in the wood, not three days past."

"I did not attack but defended. Therefore, if anyone should have a grievance, it is I, Stefan of Luften who has one against you. However, as it is that we are in a period of mourning I shall let the matter pass this once if you take your leave and promise never to enter my lands again."

The man thought for a moment. "I can see how this could be a delicate time. Have you not then taken the crown Stefan, Prince of Luften?"

"It's only a matter of timing," replied Ivan. "My brother will take the crown as king once our father has been laid to rest."

"Makes sense. Wouldn't want to be too hasty lest someone think you aided in your father's untimely demise."

Stefan's grip tightened on his battle-axe. "Leave. Now. Lest I lose my patience."

"I would. Truly, I would go if I myself did not wish to throw in my right to *Ret Til At Herske*."

Stefan swallowed hard.

"You have some balls coming here and challenging my brother to the right to rule this kingdom," Ivan bellowed.

The man shrugged. "It is my right as the heir to another kingdom. If you do not want to honor the old code, I am happy to end this in bloodshed. My men are prepared to fight. Are yours?"

Stefan's heart thundered. He should've killed the man when he'd had the chance. Last time he'd only won by a fluke. Fighting Marius again, Stefan had no idea who would win. Stefan looked down at his men, so prepared to fight for what they believed in. So ready to follow his lead. It was his duty to do the same for them.

Stefan looked to Ivan. "If the men fight, they lose. This is the only way."

Ivan grabbed Stefan's arm. "No. He has no right to ask this."

"He has every right, brother."

"But that ritual hasn't been used since the time of our grandfather."

"Any kingdom that does not have a rightful ruler is subject for any royal to challenge for the crown."

"A law made by our grandfather as a way to conquer lesser kingdoms who dare not oppose."

"Then it is only fitting that it should come back on our heads."

"If you win against my brother you will then have to fight me next," Ivan yelled.

"And I am prepared to do so," Marius replied.

"Stefan! Stop!"

Stefan turned to see Jak running toward him. Damn her. How had she gotten out? The men moved out of her way as she stormed up the steps to the gate.

"I thought you locked her in," said Ivan.

"He did!" Jak pushed Ivan aside and stood at Stefan's feet, fire burning in her steely gaze.

The sight turned him on more than he was ready to admit. If they'd been anywhere else, he'd have rushed her to his bed right then.

"How dare you lock me in."

"I didn't want you in the middle of this."

She poked him in the chest, but he couldn't feel it through his armor. "In case you haven't noticed, I am the one who single-handedly saved your rear out here."

"But—"

She held up her hand to him. "I am as much a part of this fight now as you are, so don't even try to stop me."

Stefan looked to Ivan for help, but Ivan stared at Jak bewildered.

The men below began to laugh. "You let a tiny woman

order you about? No wonder Luften has become such a dung heap."

"If it's such a dung heap, why do you want it?" Jak retorted.

"Jak, please—"

"Maybe I want it for you. I could use a woman with some spirit to keep my feet warm at night. You'd make a wonderful pet."

"I'll take your head before you lay a hand on her," Stefan yelled.

Marius smiled. "When I take the crown of Luften, bedding your little wench will be the first thing I'm sure to do. Show her what a real Jätte feels like between her legs."

Anger raged through Stefan and without thinking he bounded the rampart to the ground below. He rushed Marius, bashing him in the chest and knocking him to the ground. Prentis jumped on Stefan's back and pulled him off.

"Hell no!" Before Stefan could stop him, Ivan followed suit and jumped to the ground running at Prentis.

JAK STOOD ANGERED, ASHAMED AND TERRIFIED ALL AT THE same time as Stefan and Marius' battle-axes clashed in a spark of metal. The army stepped back as Ivan fought Prentis and Stefan battled Marius. Jak pulled on her magic, unsure of what to do. If she intervened, she had no idea what it might mean to the fight, the kingdom or Stefan.

Round and round the men went. Sometimes one getting in a blow, sometimes another. Jak stood on the gate, surrounded by the Luften men looking on and cheering for Ivan and Stefan.

Jak's grip grew tighter on the railing as she watched Ivan duck a war hammer swing above his head. He spun behind Prentis and bashed him in the back of the skull with the handle of his axe. Prentis went down face first straight into the dirt like a felled tree. Ivan kicked Prentis once, but the man didn't move. Jak pulled on the greenery under the ground and wrapped Prentis tight with the roots from her newly born trees until he resembled a fly in a spiderweb.

Stefan swung at Marius with his battle-axe and missed. Marius stuck out his foot and tripped Stefan while shoving him in the chest. Stefan fell on his back, and Marius jumped on top, axe raised.

Jak cried out, and Stefan turned to her his eyes full of sorrow. Her heart thundered as time slowed. The axe lowered toward Stefan's head. Ivan dove at Marius' legs. As he did, a soldier ran at Ivan, club raised ready to crack Ivan's skull.

Jak screamed and threw her hands out, unleashing her magick. Vines flew from the hedges and snaked around Marius' axe as well as the soldier's club. Pulling with the vines, the weapons flew through the air and landed at the gate.

Everyone stared up at Jak.

"Interference," the man yelled. "Interference is punishable by death."

Stefan pushed Marius off and hopped to his feet. "She doesn't know our laws. She isn't from here."

Marius spat blood on the ground. "The law is the law. Deliver her now."

Stefan steeled his shoulders. "No. You can take me, but you will not have her."

The man raised his hand. "Ready arrows."

Dozens of arrows lit with fire and pointed toward the village. Jak's chest squeezed.

"Deliver her or we'll burn Luften to the ground."

"Stop!" Jak cried. She reached out and an enormous Plumum tree near the gate bent a branch toward her. She stepped on and it lowered her to the ground.

"You want me?" Jak strode forward. "Come and take me."

Marius motioned for several of his men to engage her. Both Ivan and Stefan stepped in front of her, weapons at the ready. Behind her, Jätte dropped from the gate surrounding her.

Marius smiled. "Then it is to be war."

He signaled and the arrows released into the trees and beyond into Luften. Jak turned to see several of her beloved friends catch fire. "Get water!" Stefan yelled to the men at the gate.

Marius ordered more arrows to be lit. Jak's pulse drummed in her head and she pulled her magic in tight around her like a bubble as anger spurred her forward. She touched the ground and it began to quake as she pulled the trees toward her. Their roots lengthened and burst from the ground surrounding her.

Stefan, Ivan, and the others backed away as she yanked on her magic, her gaze never leaving Marius.

"You dare to shoot at my trees?"

Jak's magick swirled like a breathing, pulsing shroud tight around her. The air shimmered and crackled with light as she sucked more energy from the forest she'd created, but instead of pushing it outward to assault as she usually did, this time she gathered it closer. She sucked it in and clustered it inside her muscles. The threads of life thrummed in her veins. It snapped like lightning, tasting metallic and raw. It smelled of water churning in a waterfall and echoed like a great rush of wind in her ears. She forced it through her entire body as she moved toward him. Every muscle in her body strained with life, strengthened by her forest children.

With every step Jak took, her body stretched and strained to absorb the magic and multiplied it. Finally, she stood nose to nose with Marius, her height the same as his. Jak grabbed him with the roots of her trees and held him off the ground in front of her. His men yelled in terror and turned tail. Jak stared at Marius' shocked face.

"You shall leave Luften. And you shall tell every Jätte you come in contact with that Luften is under my protection. Anyone who has the desire to hurt any man, beast or tree in Luften will have to go through me." Her voice echoed around her louder than she'd ever heard before. Deeper and older. The voice of the guardian of the trees.

Marius swallowed hard.

"And if you ever again set foot here, I will have Stefan finish what was begun back in the forest. Do we understand each other?"

Marius nodded, wide-eyed.

Jak stared at him for a moment longer and then released him. He tumbled to the ground and backed away.

Stefan stepped beside her. "Your men have fled. I suggest you take Prentis and head the same direction."

Marius grabbed Prentis by the collar of his tunic and Jak signaled the plants to retreat. He unwrapped like a Yuletide present and Marius dragged him away.

The group continued to watch until they could no longer see him. When he was out of sight, Ivan turned to her.

"How long have you been able to get this big?"

Jak chuckled. It was strange to be able to look him in the eye for once.

"I don't know," she replied. "I guess I just needed something to give me a reason to grow beyond my form."

She turned to Stefan. "Are you hurt?"

He shook his head. "I'll be fine."

"You were willing to sacrifice your life for me."

He touched her cheek. "As you were for me."

She smiled. "Technically I was protecting my trees, but yes, you were part of it as well."

He looked over her and down at the roots that they stood on.

"My mother said I'd not even begun to tap into the powers I possessed. I suppose she was right."

As the Jätte doused the fires in the trees she headed to the affected greenery. She laid her palms on them in turn, healing their wounds and forming new life where the old fell off. With each tree she let a piece of her anger and magick release until she shrunk back to her usual form.

When the last of her trees had been healed, she walked to the gate where Stefan and Ivan were busy setting up a watch to guard the gate and more in the towers to make sure they had no more surprise visitors. They set several to task taking care of the fully blossomed fields and more to continue in the repairs of the keep and huts. Though they'd avoided war, Stefan did not mean to give the men time to be idle.

An hour after the men were set to task, Jak ordered Ivan and Stefan up to the keep to have their wounds tended to.

On the long walk back Jak realized something had changed inside her. The way she'd communed with her trees. The way she'd healed them and they had helped her in return. A bond had forged that could not be broken. There was no turning back. She'd not found her place, but created it instead. Until the day she died, she would protect her trees, Luften, and those inside. She was home.

CHAPTER FOURTEEN

The next few days passed in a blur for Stefan as the men hurried to fortify the kingdom. They buried his father, and he was bestowed the crown of Luften. The men had celebrated and paid homage to both Stefan as well as his father, leaving little time for Stefan to be with Jak. Not that she'd been in Luften. After the unexplained happenings on the battlefield, Jak had gone to see her mother for answers. She'd stayed away two days and just as he'd begun to worry about her and Pasha, they'd returned, tired and hungry.

She'd slept most of the day, but as evening approached and the men were winding down for the night, Stefan climbed the stairs to their rooms to check on her.

The whole atmosphere of Luften had changed with the passing of his father. As if a shroud had lifted off the kingdom and life had breathed into it once more. Stefan was keenly aware that that life had come not from him or his brother, but from Jak. He wondered what would happen if Jak chose to go back to the low ground.

Stefan reached his chamber when Ivan caught up with him.

"Brother. It's here."

Stefan stared at Ivan for a long moment unable to speak for the dread that rained down on him. The stalk had returned. It seemed a lifetime since Jak had arrived and no more than a moment at the same time.

"Shall I go alone?"

Stefan shook his head. "I'll get you when I'm ready. We shall go together and reclaim all that this Rupert has stolen from us."

"Are we to kill him then? Exact revenge?"

Stefan shook his head. "I was thinking more along the lines of repaying his debt."

"I would like to see that very much."

Stefan threw him a tight smile and Ivan's gaze traveled to the door.

"You don't have to tell her," said Ivan. "We can tell her that with everything going on we didn't realize it."

Stefan shook his head. "Didn't you promise Jak that there would be no more lies between you?"

Ivan smiled, clapped him on the back, and headed toward his room. "Well, maybe this can be the very last one."

Stefan blew out a long breath and then entered his chamber. The sound of water splashing caught his attention. He ran his fingers through his hair. He couldn't not tell her the stalk had returned. The choice to stay must be hers and hers alone. To take that from her would go against everything he believed in.

"Jak?" he called. "I need to speak with you."

There was a pause and then, "I'll be right out."

Stefan rested on his bed, listening to the sounds of the water moving as Jak got out of the tub, and the patter of her small feet as she crossed her room. She stopped by the door that separated them. Her peachy skin flushed from the warmth of the bath. Her wet hair hung a deeper shade down her naked arms and back.

"Is something wrong?"

He didn't want to voice the words. He wanted to let the night pass as if nothing was out of the ordinary. To give them more time. Her more time to acclimate.

"The stalk is back," he blurted.

She gave him a mild smile. "I am aware. It told me."

"Told you?"

"My mother has shown me many things in the past days. How to feel the life around me is just one of the things. I sensed the stalk coming for the past two days. It reached out to me this morning."

"You're connected to the stalk?"

"My mother created the stalk as a way for me to come home. Little did she know how that would happen when she did so."

Stefan couldn't see the logic in the theory. "Wouldn't it have been better if she'd gone to you? I mean, the likelihood you would find your way to the stalk and climb up is pretty remote."

"And yet, here I stand."

Stefan nodded. The sight of her in her towel flooded his body with interest.

"So...."

Her eyebrows drew together. "So?"

"The stalk will only be here until midnight."

She nodded. "Yes."

"I just thought you should know, in case..."

"In case what?"

"In case you wanted to leave."

She blinked several times. "You wish me to go?"

"No." Stefan got to his feet. "That's not what I meant."

"Then what did you mean?"

"I just... I wanted to make sure you knew you are free to leave whenever you see fit."

She snickered. "If I wanted to leave, I would have gone already."

A lightning strike of hope bolted through him. "So, you want to stay?"

Without a word she unwrapped her towel, letting it drop to her feet. Stefan swallowed hard as his breeches grew so tight he feared they might burst.

He took in her creamy curves. The swell of her small breasts. The slight jutting of her hipbones. The slender silkiness of her thighs and the hair between them that matched the hair of her head.

She crept toward him; her hands clenched at her sides. With every step, she grew larger and larger until she stood at his shoulder, her form more significant and yet still as delicate.

"So, you can... do that now? Whenever you want?"

Her hands found their way under the hem of his tunic, and she tugged it up over his head and tossed it to the floor.

"My mother showed me how. Once my Illumis tree has sprouted and grown, I will be able to do a great many things."

He slid his hand around her waist feeling her soft skin beneath his palm. She ran her fingers up his abdomen to his chest and swirled her fingers in the thick hair covering the healing bruises from his fight.

"Do they still hurt?"

She leaned in close and kissed his chest. His hands tightened on her hips at the touch of her mouth on his skin.

Stefan's voice came out raspy. "Not so much."

She ran her tongue over his collarbone and up the side of his throat, making his hardening length twitch with need.

"Jak..."

She kissed across his chin to the other side of his throat. "Stefan..."

His hand slid downward to her bare rear, cupping and kneading her soft flesh. He wanted her. More than anything in the world he wanted her.

"Jak..."

She reached down between his legs and rubbed him through his breeches.

"Stefan..."

His restraint broke. He kissed her hard, plunging his tongue into her mouth. She pushed back equally as hard taking in every sweep of his tongue. Stefan lifted Jak off the floor and carried her to his bed. He pushed back the blankets and laid her down. Stripping off his boots and breeches he climbed on top of her. It was strange to have her so vast yet so right at the same time. He kissed her again and then ran his tongue down her throat between her breasts. Her fingers tangled in his hair as he kissed her hipbones in turn and proceeded lower. He kissed down the inside of her left thigh allowing her scent to linger on his skin.

She pulled his mouth back up to meet hers and ran her hand down his body, guiding him towards her. He stopped just shy of entering her.

She lay back on the pillow. "What's wrong?"

"I don't want to hurt you."

She caressed his cheek. "Go slow."

He nodded and kissed her again. His body wound tighter at the impending sense of release. He circled her soft curls, trying to warm her to the idea of him. She pushed her hips closer to his. He kissed down to her breasts and circled her nipple with his tongue before reaching down between them and running his fingers between her soft folds. Her breath caught, and her fingers dug deep into his shoulders.

JAK'S BODY PULSED WITH MAGIC, LIFE AND NEED. TOO MANY days had passed since she'd kissed Stefan and felt his hands on her. She'd known at that moment that she would never belong to another, but things had needed to be done. He'd needed time to mourn and bury his father, and she'd needed time to see her mother. Yesenia had taught her how to harness the power inside her; and instead of giving it to her plants, using for herself to increase her stature so she could rival that of the Jätte.

As Stefan's fingers slipped inside her, she bucked her hips. Strange at first the sensation grew into one of pleasure as she'd never known. She bit down on his bottom lip causing him to moan. Grabbing onto his shoulders as he poised at her entrance she rocked forward gently. He paused waiting.

"Keep going," she commanded.

He pressed forward inch by inch until he filled her. She breathed deep and kissed him hard. Running her hands down his back to his firm buttocks she cupped him as he withdrew and then slid into her again. Pleasure rocked through Jak as she lay back. Sensations skittered across her skin raising goosebumps, making her beg for more. Her gaze connected with his as his body moved against hers, rubbing her and sending her into spirals of pleasure she'd never known. Stefan's rhythm increased, as did the friction between them until his body tensed and his head whipped backward as he called her name. Jak pulled him through his climax as her body relished the connection between them. His body slacked and he fell on top of her, kissing down her throat.

He gazed at her and pushed her hair from her face before kissing her softly.

"I love you, Jakleen."

She cupped his cheek. "And I you, Stefan."

He kissed her again and then withdrew. "Come. Let me bathe you and show you the same pleasure you have shown me this night."

"And tomorrow?" she teased

He kissed her. "And the next."

"And the next?"

He stared deep into her eyes. "And forever my dearest, my love, my queen."

CHAPTER FIFTEEN

Jak slid along the side of the large house and pointed at the front door. Stefan nodded to Ivan, and the brothers strode toward it without fear of reprisal or discovery.

Stefan stepped aside and motioned for Ivan. "After you."

Ivan grinned and kicked the front door in.

Jak glanced up and down the street watching for any onlookers. A cry floated out the front door, and the sounds of crashing breakables echoed through the night. Another cry sounded and then a thud.

Jak glanced at the door but could see nothing in the darkness. Voices sounded from the huts all around as lights flickered on.

Stefan stepped outside, a hogtied Rupert slung over his shoulder. "We should go."

"Where's Ivan?"

"Gathering our stolen wealth."

Jak nodded. "There are just two more stops."

Jak marched toward her hut, head held high. She no longer feared her father nor what he would say. Opening the front door, she allowed the chilly wind to snuff out the meager fire that burned in the fireplace. Jak glanced around the hut. Food, trash, and filth had accumulated in the little time she'd been gone. She shook her head and made her way to her father's bed. He snored loudly, draped across the frame. Anger bubbled inside Jak.

She reached out with her boot and kicked his foot. "Hey."

He snorted but did not wake.

She kicked him harder. "Wake up."

Her father moaned and rolled over eyeing her blinkingly. "Where the hell have you been?"

"Where is the butterfly comb that Rupert gave you?"

"What?" He rubbed his face.

"Where is the butterfly comb that Rupert offered you and told you to give to me?"

"I... it... uh..." He sat in a stupor for a moment. "I sold it."

"To whom?"

Her father leaped from his bed suddenly. "Where have you been? Do you know the mess you've made? The trouble you've caused?" He reached for her, but she pulled away. He advanced, and she backed to the door. "Rupert has been furious. He cut me off. The tavern cut me off. Everyone has cut me off, and it's all because of you."

Jak stepped outside the hut, and her father stumbled out after her.

"You owe me girl, and you are going to pay for what you've cost me."

Jak stopped moving and looked her father dead in the eyes. "You think I owe you something? That you are due some compensation?"

"Yes."

She nodded. "Then I think perhaps that is something you might want to take up with someone."

Stefan stepped out of the shadows and loomed over Jak's father. Her father's face paled, and he stumbled away.

"Father, I'd like for you to meet King Stefan of Luften, my husband."

Stefan stepped forward and yanked Jak's father off the ground. "I know what you have done to Jak. The way you've used her. Abused her. Sold her. And I tell you now. If you ever coming looking for Jak, it will be the last anyone hears from you. Am I clear?"

Her father nodded frantically.

"Now, where is my mother's hair comb?"

He father swallowed hard. "I...I...I... sold it to the tavern owner."

Stefan dropped Jak's father and turned toward the trees. "Tavern," he called.

Ivan tossed Rupert to Galin. "Take him and lock him up."

Galin nodded and lumbered back through the wood. When Ivan and Stefan had asked for a volunteer to go with them and help set things right, Galin was the first to volunteer. He'd done nothing but try to show both Jak and Stefan how sorry he was for helping kidnap Jak in the past weeks. Though Jak no longer blamed him as she saw the bigger picture of his actions.

Ivan looked down at Jak's father. "Fee, Fi, Foe, Fum, I smell the blood of a cowardly man." He stomped forward as if to grab Jak's father and her father scampered into the hut, slamming the door behind him.

Ivan chuckled. "As if that would stop me if I really wanted to eat him."

Jak took Stefan's hand and pulled him away from the hut. "You head toward the stalk. I just have one more stop."

"I should come with you."

She shook her head. "I'll get the comb and then I'll join you both shortly."

Stefan bent and kissed her head. "Thirty minutes. Then I come looking."

She nodded and turned back toward town.

Stefan pulled her to a stop. "Husband?"

Jak shrugged. "Do you not want to be my husband?"

A broad smile stretched across his face, and he cupped her chin in his hand. "More than anything."

Jak nodded. "Good. Because I want to be your wife." She smiled and then headed off toward the Ugly Ogre.

"Thirty minutes," Stefan called.

JAK WALKED UP THE PATH TO THE SMALL HUT AT THE EDGE of the cliff. She patted the butterfly comb in her pocket just to make sure she hadn't dropped it, though she knew she had not. She didn't want to leave anything on the low ground that would force her to have to come back.

The garden she'd grown blossomed and flourished making her smile as she strode to the door and knocked lightly.

She waited several moments and then knocked again.

"Who is it?" Olivia's voice came out soft and afraid.

"Jak."

Olivia opened the door slowly. "I've been so worried. I heard in town that you had been missing for over two weeks. Where have you been?"

Jak held out her hand to Olivia. "Would you like to see?"

Olivia opened the door wider and looked Jak up and down. "Now?"

Jak nodded. "There isn't much time. We have to leave. You can come back if you wish, not for a couple of weeks, but trust me Olivia, you aren't going to want to come back. Not when you see what I've found."

Olivia grabbed her cloak off the peg by the door and wrapped it around her shoulders before stepping outside and taking Jak's hand.

"What is it? What have you found?" she asked.

"You'll see. We must hurry though, or we'll be stuck down here."

"Down here?"

Jak pulled Olivia around the cliffs to the far side and stopped as the stalk came into view.

"Wh... what is that?" Olivia whispered.

Jak urged her forward. "The beanstalk."

They stopped just in front of it and Jak allowed Olivia a moment to take in the immensity of the plant.

A rustle sounded behind them and Olivia cried out as Stefan stepped from the shadows.

"Don't worry," Jak soothed. "He's with me. This is my soon-to-be husband, King Stefan of Luften."

Stefan stepped up and took Jak's hand.

Olivia looked between them, her expression a mixture of wonder and fear.

"We must go my love," said Stefan. "It is nearly midnight."

Jak nodded. "Come with us, Olivia."

Olivia looked up at Stefan and then the stalk and finally Jak again.

"I won't let anything happen to you," Jak promised.

"Nor I," said Stefan.

"Nor I," said Ivan.

Olivia flattened herself against the stalk and reached for something in her cloak but there was nothing in it.

"Jak—"

She held her hand up to Stefan. "You go. We'll be right behind."

He looked to Ivan and then kissed Jak's hand and began to climb.

Olivia watched him for a moment and then looked to Jak. "I don't think I can climb that far."

"I can carry you," Ivan offered.

Jak squeezed Olivia's hand. "This is Prince Ivan, Stefan's brother. I trust him with my life as well as yours."

Jak grabbed the stalk and reached out to one of the

smaller winding vines. It unfurled a large leaf and Jak sat upon it.

"I promise to keep you safe," Ivan said in a gentle tone Jak had never heard from him before. "And if you want to come back, I will bring you back myself in a fortnight."

Jak commanded the vine to carry her upward and she ascended the stalk as Ivan picked up Olivia.

"I get the feeling that won't be necessary." Olivia said as Ivan set her on his back. "I don't have anything left here."

"That makes both of us," Ivan replied.

Jak smiled to herself. She gave a silent prayer of thanks to her mother for making the stalk. She had the feeling that hers wasn't the only life that would be changed by the creation.

THE END

OLIVIA AND THE GIANT

FAIRELLE BOOK NINE

By Rebekah R. Ganiere

CHAPTER ONE

LUFTEN, JÄTTE KINGDOM - EARLY SPRING, 1213 A.D. (AFTER DAEMONS)

Olivia walked behind the Jätte inspecting the set of their arms, the level of their bows and the placement of their stance. She stopped behind Ivan as he pulled the bow string taut. She set her hands on his shoulders and squared them slightly.

He grumbled.

"If you didn't want my help, you shouldn't have come when I'm working with the others," she whispered.

Ivan loosed his arrow and it hit just right of the bullseye.

"See," Olivia teased. "If I hadn't helped you would have missed completely."

Ivan blew out a harsh breath. "I'm better with a melee weapon. I was built for hand to hand combat."

"Yes. But what was the point of Jak growing a forest around Luften to keep it safe if you are just going to run straight out into the fray and get yourself killed?"

He notched another arrow. "What does it matter? Since

the growing of the Luften Forest we've not had a single Jätte challenge us."

Olivia scanned the combat area, and her gaze moved to the outer gate. "True. But you've had many men move here."

Ivan followed her gaze.

A group of Jätte women rode through the gates on steeds much larger than what Olivia was used to. She'd tried only once since arriving in Luften to ride the beasts but she'd been terrified and almost thrown. The group of Jätte women slowed as they passed the combat training grounds. The men straightened and smiled. All except Ivan who scowled and shook his head.

"Most likely because of them," he grumbled.

Olivia hadn't been able to work out exactly why he disliked the women coming in search of husbands, and she hadn't dared ask.

The women looked at her suspiciously and then turned and continued on.

"More mouths to feed. Wonderful." Ivan loosed his arrow and it sailed over the target.

"Surely there is enough now that everyone has started trading with Luften again. The fruits and vegetables you grow rival even those of Ville DeFee- but on a much larger scale of course. I honestly never even knew that tomatoes could grow as large as my head."

Ivan loosed three arrows in quick succession and hit the other side of the bullseye. He swore under his breath.

"And where were those helpful Jätte when we were in dire need? Charging twice as much as we afford and giving us only the lowest of quality that they couldn't sell anyone else."

Olivia understood the feeling of being taken advantage of all too well. After leaving Ville DeFee there had been many a shopkeeper who were willing to take advantage of a lone female. It had been one of the reasons she'd agreed to go with Jak up the beanstalk. That and the fact that if there had been even the minutest degree of a chance that she could find a place she felt she fit in, she was willing to take it.

"Oye! Watch that yer' doin'," said Barron. "You'll kill someone if ya don't pay attention."

Olivia walked across the ramp that had been built, allowing her to reach the same height as the Jätte.

"What's going on?" she asked like a scolding mother.

"He's not paying attention and almost shot one of the chickens."

"I did not," said Rufus. "I'm no better than I was two months ago, which means I couldn't hit that chicken if it was the size of Pasha."

"All right," Olivia announced. "Why don't we take a break from archery for today. Grab something to eat and if you want to come back later we can practice axe throwing."

The men took their bows and walked them to the rack. Only Ivan continued to practice.

"Aren't you hungry?" she asked.

Ivan shot the arrow and it landed in the target a hair off the bullseye.

"You know that's good enough, right? You can still kill someone if you hit them slightly to the side of the heart."

"I won't stop until I can do it as well as you. What kind

of Jätte would I be if I wasn't at least as good as a Low Ground woman?"

"Is that a challenge or an insult?"

Ivan stopped and looked at her and for a moment his eyes changed and all anger fled from his face.

"Neither. At least it wasn't meant as such. I apologize. It's just…" His gaze traveled to the castle.

Olivia sat on the wooden ramp. Ivan didn't talk much she noticed so it surprised her that he talked to her quite frequently. But then she'd always been a good listener. For Rome, Cinder, even her mother. She swallowed hard at the thought of her mother.

"What's got you so riled up today?" she asked. "Did Stefan best you at wrestling again?"

"No."

Ivan set his bow next to her and looked at her hard for a moment. He crossed his arms over his large chest and chewed his lip. She knew better than to try and coax words out of him. He would say what he needed to say, but it always had to be Ivan's decision to do it. She'd learned that about him all too well.

"Stefan wants me to dress up and entertain the females coming to Luften. He wants me to settle down and take a wife," he finally said.

"And… you don't want to?"

"No. I mean yes. I mean…ugh. I don't know. Do I want a wife? Sure. If the right woman came along. But I don't want to settle down and marry someone just because my brother tells me I should. He thinks if I marry a woman from another kingdom, possibly a princess or some other royal that it will solidify our kingdom and gain us allies."

For some reason Olivia's stomach clenched at the thought. She wasn't sure why but something about what she'd just been told didn't sit right with her.

"Does Luften need solidifying?" she asked.

"Not as far as I'm concerned. And in all honesty, if my brother had been so concerned about it, he should have married a princess from another kingdom not make me do it. Why would I want a princess anyway? What the hell would I do with her?"

"You could learn to dance."

He looked at her quizzically. "What?"

"Dance. Down in Fairelle the princes always have balls where they meet eligible females to marry. You could learn to dance and have a ball."

"And you think a princess would like a prince who can dance?"

Olivia shrugged. "Sure. It would show you are refined."

"Well that's settled then." Ivan picked up his bow, notched another arrow and pulled his string taut.

"What is?"

"Dancing." He loosed the arrow and it flew dead center of the bullseye. "If dancing and balls are what princesses want, then I absolutely refuse to do it." He turned back to her, set down his bow and picked up his battle axe.

Olivia smiled and hopped down from her ramp. "Well then, if you aren't going to learn to dance then maybe you can do something more useful."

"And what would that be Little Bit?"

She hefted a battle axe the size and make of the one Ivan held. In her hands it weighed no more than a few loaves of bread. There were a great many things Olivia had learned about herself since being separated from her mother and her mother's restrictive magick. Her greater than average strength being just one of those things.

She walked into the fighting arena and turned to him. "Well, are you coming? Or do I need to find someone else to spar with?"

A smile spread across his face as he lumbered toward her. "What if you get hurt?"

Olivia returned his smile and stepped into a defensive stance. "Don't worry. I heal quicker than you'd think."

"I don't want to hurt you."

She smiled broader. "Now where's the fun in that?" Without waiting she launched herself at him.

Olivia and the Giant Is Coming Soon!

THANK YOU

Thank you for taking the time to read
Jak the Giant Healer. This one was tricky for me because I
wasn't quite sure how I would work out their size difference.
But I love how it turned out. I hope you did too.

If you enjoyed the book, please take a moment to leave a
review on your favorite retailer.

To find out more about **Rebekah R. Ganiere** and her
other Upcoming Releases, Join her Street Team
or for Swag and Freebies, Please connect with her in the
following places:
Rebekah R. Ganiere - BOOKS WITH A BITE
www.RebekahGaniere.com/Newsletter

Award Winning–*USA Today* Bestselling Author

Rebekah R. Ganiere

Fairelle Series

Red the Were Hunter - Book One

Yanti's Choice - Fairelle Short Story

Snow the Vampire Slayer - Book Two

Jamen's Yuletide Bride - Book Three

Zelle and the Tower - Book Four

Cinder the Fae - Book Five

Belle and the Beast - Book Six

Gerall's Festivus Bride - Book Seven

Jak the Giant Healer - Book Eight

Wolf River

PROMISED at the Moon

CURSED by the Moon

RECLAIMED from the Moon

TAMED under the Moon

UNLEASHED with the Moon

FATED despite the Moon

The Society Series

Reign of the Vampires

Rise of the Fae

Vengeance of the Demons

The Otherworlder Series

Saving Christmas

Cupid's Curse

Kissed by the Reaper

Dracula's Bride

Rekindling Christmas

Christmas Lodge (2020)

Dead Awakenings (2020)

NEWSLETTER

To claim your Two **FREE** Books and find out more about
Rebekah R. Ganiere and her other Upcoming Releases
You can Go Here:
www.RebekahGaniere.com/Newsletter

www.ingramcontent.com/pod-product-compliance
Lightning Source LLC
Chambersburg PA
CBHW020908180626
46816CB00007BA/2308